"What I love about Jon Nix as a writer is that he does not flinch. These stories are quietly stunning world-builders that are revelatory by the end, whether in the aftermath of a burst pipe or during a man's bludgeoning. Nix writes with such concise clarity that when the violence and joy show up, you feel it in your guts."

– James Croal Jackson, author of *A God You Believed In*

"Mesmerizing and immersive, Ferals is a portal into the complex specificity of working-class survival. We meet characters who are all at once enigmatic and familiar, abhorrent and also deeply sympathetic. Reading this was nothing short of an experience, dropping me into the thick heat of a Florida summer---rarely have I encountered such richly evocative and atmospheric writing. Nix is proving himself as one of the most compelling storytellers of our time."

–Raechel Anne Jolie, author of *Rust Belt Femme*

"These stories are grimy and badass and make me feel like nothing could ever possibly be good again. I love them."

– Nick Gregorio, author of *Launch Me to the Stars,*
I'm Finished Here

www.withanxbooks.com
Cover Design by Steak MTN
Layout by Jon Nix
WAX008
ISBN 979-8-9874787-5-2

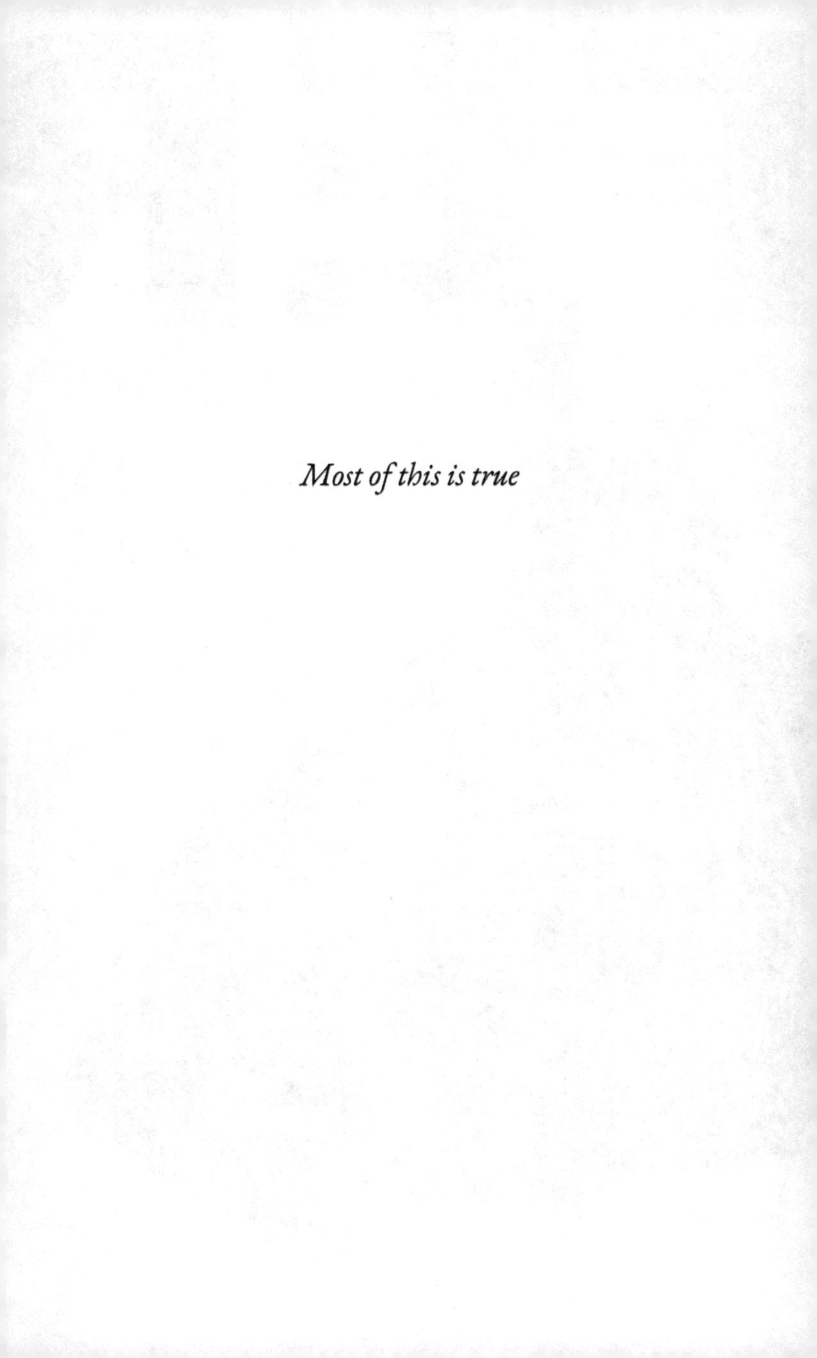

Most of this is true

FER

ALS

JON NIX

MMXXIV

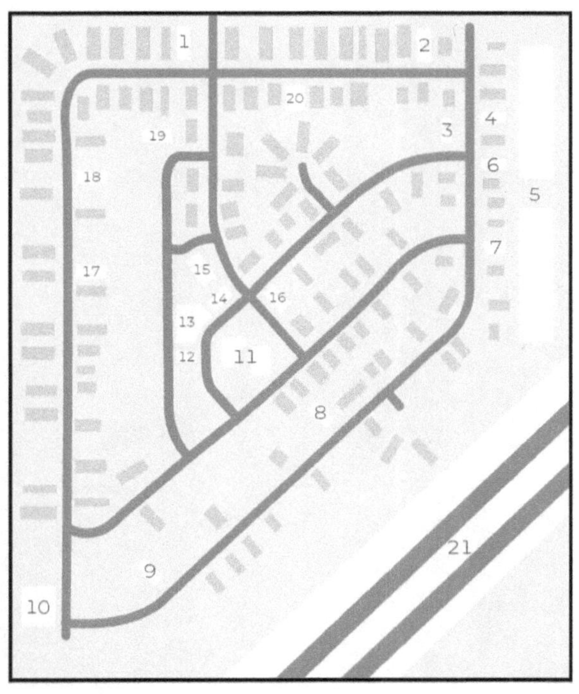

1. Chuck's Lot
2. Bill's Lot
3. Joe's Lot
4. Andrew's Lot
5. Storm Ditch
6. David's Lot
7. Danny's Lot
8. Jogger's Lot
9. Sam's Lot
10. Junk Heap
11. Clubhouse & Pool
12. Dumpster
13. Playground
14. Mailboxes
15. Manager's Lot
16. Blowjob House
17. Seth's Lot
18. Kim's Lot
19. Jake's Lot
20. Chris' Lot
21. Highway

LONG SHADOWS

Andrew rarely noticed when it happened, but when he was lost in thought, he'd cross his arms and run his fingers along the ridges of his ribs. He'd walk home past darkened windows, free hand swatting at mosquitoes, watching his shadow grow longer behind him as he approached each streetlight.

The boys would edge each other into staying out past curfew. Sometimes they would say their goodbyes and when no one walked away they would continue on as if nothing happened. During the summer they liked to stay out past dusk. When the air stayed warm well into the night. Their eyes would be tired, sore from all of the chlorine in the community pool. They would rub their eyes and stare up at the streetlights and catch beautiful light flares they could only see after a long day of swimming.

Andrew came from a long line of night owls. When they were young, his father and uncle were known as the 42 Cat-Killers. 42nd street was always lousy with strays. They crawled up under the hoods of cars to stay warm. When the engines turned over the cat's would get sucked into the belts and be torn to shreds, coating the engine in fur and red. The brothers would sneak through their neighborhood at night killing stray cats and collecting money from grateful neighbors. Andrew never knew his father but his uncle would come over and tell him stories. His uncle told him about how his dad was the best at killing those strays. His hands would look enormous to Andrew, as he would mime what it looked like when his dad broke their necks. Andrew looked down at his hands, his skinny wrists, unable to picture himself doing something like that.

On the nights he stayed over, his uncle would drink until he'd black out and shoot his gun off at dawn before collapsing. He'd wake up sunburnt and dehydrated, with fire ants crawling up the hairs on his calf. Those nights made Andrew uncomfortable. He'd see glances pass between his mom and his uncle that he couldn't understand. They'd tell him it was bedtime and as he laid there he could hear them whispering. Every so often his mom would giggle loudly, and then what sounded like a hand covering her mouth, muffled the sound.

The thing that fascinated Andrew the most about his uncle was the way he cleaned his fingernails with a pocket knife. He'd watch his uncle snap his knife open, one-handed, and slide it under each nail without ever looking away from the tv. One day Andrew tried it himself. He plucked the knife from his uncle's Wranglers. The handle was mother of pearl with olive green detailing. With some effort, he got the hinge to give and the knife snapped open. He took it in his hand and wrapped a fist around the handle, making some stabbing motions. Then he nestled the tip of the blade under the corner of his thumbnail and began to drag. The blade slipped deep under his thumbnail. He dropped the knife and held the nail down until his skin turned white to stop the bleeding. They'd been out of band-aids and so a makeshift bandage was made from a folded paper towel and scotch tape. Over the next few days, Andrew watched with growing concern at the red line crawling up his finger. He didn't know what a staph infection looked like but he knew something was wrong. When the red line crept all the way to his knuckle he caved and showed his mom. Without hesitation she held his hand under the bathroom faucet and peeled his nail back to wash out the pus as he thrashed between her legs.

SPEED BUMPS

It was a typical Florida trailer park. The nicer trailers were all strategically placed near the entrance. The doublewides and the freshly painted ones owned by families with some cash to spare. Once you entered the park you came to a t-junction. If you followed the loop to the right you'd swing around back and end up near the junk heap and the area where the trailers thinned out. If you went left, you'd end up by the drainage ditches. Most people who moved in considered it a step up since the streets were paved and there was a small pool and playground that everyone had access to.

A few years after we moved into the trailer park a new manager took over. One who cared. He had speed bumps put in to make it safer for the kids who played in the street. It was no secret that the people who lived there would drink and drive. And if he couldn't keep them from drinking he'd at least slow them down when they came barreling in at three in the morning.

The kicker was that the speed bumps were poured too high. If cars drove over them at any kind of speed it would tear up the bottom of the car. One time a whole exhaust was ripped from a car. We heard a scraping sound followed by a deafening engine roar, and then a man screaming "Fuck!" over and over. I went to the window and saw him kicking his car door in. Now that I'm older I assume it's because he already knew the car was totalled. Why hesitate in adding to the damage? After months of complaints and a handful of legal battles the manager agreed to fix the situation. He drove his tractor out at dawn that morning, grinder attachment hooked to the front. The timing was spite on his part. If everyone wanted this so bad then he felt they could wake up as early as he did. One by one he grinded down the asphalt mounds, already sticky in the morning sun. By the end of the day, every one of them was half their previous size, with long gash marks like the backs of manatees.

That same day Vicky was found sometime before noon. Before the sun was all the way up and the air was heavy. A jogger passing by saw her from the street lying face down in the yard, her dress bunched up at the small of her back. She had been raped and murdered sometime in the night. The whole thing seemed to have happened less than ten feet from Andrew's room but he hadn't heard a thing. The first thing that tipped Andrew off that anything bad had happened was the glare of police lights shining through his bedroom window. He wiped the sleep from his eyes and watched the blue and red lights dance on his ceiling. Pulling the curtain back revealed officers traipsing through the yard, followed by a heavy knock at the door. That was about all he ever said to me about it.

An investigation was launched. Nothing was ever definitively solved. Not that I know of. People had ideas about what had happened. They would whisper them late at night. Amateur sleuths lit by bug zappers. Older women would gesture toward the trailer where that one boy lived, cigarettes between their acrylic tipped nails.

The park manager didn't leave for another six months but her murder was the final straw for him. He'd tried to fix the park up. Make it a good place to live. But something broke in him. One day his truck was gone without a word.

IXNAY

Kim was born with shit luck. She'd run off from her dad's house when she was seventeen. Ended up stranded in the trailer park. She shacked up with a guy named Dwayne. Dwayne did odd jobs. Most recently he'd done a month-long stretch cleaning up damage left over from a hurricane that ripped through the upper part of the state. The panhandle. Clearing debris and driving it off to a landfill, mostly. One night he and the guys headed into a small diverbar named Gatorville, just north of Orlando. Kim was sitting on a stool under the dartboard sipping a beer she'd gotten without having to flash her fake ID.

Dwayne got a beer and a set of darts from the bar. He stepped across from Kim unnoticed. She was staring into a glowing Genesee sign above the pool table. When the dark thunked into the board just over her head he had her attention.

"Hey."

Another dart, this time higher, less threatening. She looked up at the darts and then back at him.

"What's your name?"

Her blood was racing but she wasn't going to let him know.

"William Tell."

"Is that right?"

He nodded.

Kim crossed her legs. She had on daisy dukes an ankle bracelet and a toe ring. He kept his eyes from wandering down.

She craned her neck back.

"Think you can hit the eight?"

Dwayne nodded.

"Do I get your number if I do?"

"You've already got my number. Right there." She pointed up. "Eight."

Dwayne closed one eye and took aim at the board. He let the dart fly. It sank into the lower loop of the eight with a thunk.

When Kim went to give him her number she almost let the number to her dad's house slip out. Then she realized she had no number. She had no plan.

"I don't have one."

Dwayne nodded again.

"Okay, I can take a hint."

He sat the remaining darts on the pool table next to him.

"Wait a minute." She said, breaking her cool. "Where

do you live?"

They'd spend all day together lying naked on his hand-me-down couch. All the windows would be open, AC off to save money. Sometimes the boys would get the gumption to sneak up to the window and peek at what was happening. Kim would whisper things into his ear, through his long hair. Things the boys could never make out. Sometimes they'd fuck so loud you could hear the sounds in the street as you were walking by. On late summer days they'd get overheated and call it quits before either of them finished. Afterward, they would writhe on each other, mixing sweat, until he'd say: "Get up. I'm hot." He'd stomp over to the kitchen to hang his head in the open freezer.

In the winter months she'd lie on his chest, rising and falling with his breaths. Florida never got that cold. Not by anyone else's standard. But it was the only time of year that body heat didn't make her feel claustrophobic. She'd hang tight to him, breathing him in, nipping at his skin with her teeth.

She was always in short shorts. When they drove his truck to the store, she'd always flip off her shoes and throw her feet up on the dash. If she was drunk she'd end up pressing her toes into glass to hold herself steady, leaving behind oily footprints that would catch the light at sunset. She would get catcalled at red lights and snap "Fuck you pig!" as they drove away. Dwayne would laugh every time and Kim would grab his hand and rest it on her inner thigh, working him up by asking if he liked when those pigs looked at her.

On clear nights, when it decided not to pour, they'd

sit out back. Citronella candles lit, but still swatting mosquitoes. Dwayne rarely wore a shirt. When he'd grab a fresh beer from the chest he'd snag the bottom of her shirt and use it to twist off the cap. If he was feeling romantic he'd hold the cap to her lips and say: "Make a wish." She'd close her eyes and pause a moment before giving the cap a kiss. He'd rear back and wing the cap toward the drainage ditch, miming a gun with his fingers, following the little hunk of tin like he was shooting skeet. He'd turn back to her and say: "What'd you wish for, baby?" She'd grab his beer and take a swig, making eyes. She'd say: "None of your business."

One time she clamped down on his forearm with her hair straightener. And when he began screaming and calling 911, she slunk back, laughing, like she was the biggest flirt. It got so they didn't trust each other. She'd kill the headlights coming around the corner and burst through the door in hopes of finding him inside another woman. If he was home, he was drunk asleep. No beers left for her. She'd never thought much of making plans but she knew this wasn't going to last.

Panic finally set in when she found out she was pregnant. She'd been good and ready for him to demand that she abort it. But that's not what happened. He was thrilled about it. Said he'd gotten bored with the life he was living and that maybe a kid would be fun. She'd lay on the couch and listen as he suggested baby names. It was three months in when she decided to run off. She left so fast she didn't even stop to put on shoes, for fear he'd wake up and she'd chicken out. She walked barefoot to the closest pay phone at a Texaco up the street. The key pad was covered in mole crickets. It was that time of year when every humming, buzzing light would end up covered in mole crickets. She pulled off her tank top and twisted it into a rattail. Swatting them off. By the time she was dialing she'd almost forgotten how scared she was to hear her dad's voice.

CLEAN UP

Bill never got along with his father. Later in life he'd find it hard to drink in a group of people. He'd always have this sense of guilt that sat in the pit of his stomach. It'd make him nauseous if he drank a beer too quickly and he'd have to run off to the bathroom and drink water from the faucet, out of view of his friends.

The summer he turned ten was the same year his parents decided to spray paint the driveway. They thought it'd help slow the cracking under the brutal onslaught of the Florida heat. They'd gotten in a fight over how many cans they'd need and his mother came home with a bruised cheek. In the end she'd been right. They hadn't bought enough and the last can blew dry a good 3 feet from the shed in back of the carport. Neither Bill, or his mother said a word when his dad ran back out to buy more cans.

There was talk in the neighborhood of his mom getting pregnant whenever their welfare ran out. Bill had a handful of siblings. Both of his parents had kids from previous marriages. They both had shared custody and when all the kids were over they would end up sleeping on top of each other in their cramped bedroom. Bill would have to give up his bed and sleep on the floor or his older half-brother would pitch a fit.

The carpet in their trailer was dark brown and thinning in the most trafficked areas. Whenever Seth ended up at Bill's for the night he'd feel the punch of heavy cigarette smoke and never took his shoes off, afraid he'd stain his socks. Seth always went home stinking like an ashtray, and his mother would berate him, accusing him of smoking. Their parents never spoke to each other. No one's did. So there was no way of verifying his answers. She'd given up smoking 6 years prior and was nauseated by the smell. Her friends who'd quit spoke nostalgically about the smell. This never made sense to her.

Seth ended up staying at Bill's for a sleepover one night. Bill's dad chain smoked and watched Commando. Cackling every time one of the nameless, faceless villains got blown away. Afterward he ran out for a pack of cigarettes and a forty for his night cap. His mom shuffled Bill and Seth to the bathroom to get cleaned up for the night. She told them to take their bath together. Save Water. Bill protested that he was too old for that. And she just repeated: "Hurry up before your dad gets home."

They both got undressed without looking at each other. Bill was naked and filling the tub with water before Seth had even undone his pants. He was always on the shy side and got made fun of for it. Seth was relieved when he saw Bill squeezing a bottle of shampoo into the running water, filling the tub with a cover of bubbles. When he finally slunk into the tub he had his back to the faucet and he kept his hand cupped around his privates. They both shampooed and rinsed. Seth was lifting handfuls of water to his head when he noticed Bill staring. He looked down at the gap in the bubbles created by the falling water.

"What?"

Bill cocked his head, still staring. "You look different?"

Seth looked down at himself.

"Different?"

Bill looked back up to Seth.

"Yeah, different from me." Bill spread his legs to reveal his uncircumcised penis.

Seth drew back.

"What's wrong with yours?"

Bill got on his knees, gripping himself.

"Nothing, my mom says it's normal."

Seth watched as water streamed off of Bill.

"It looks funny. Does yours work different?"

Bill let go, almost showing it off.

"I don't know." Bill was thinking. "Does yours get hard too?"

"Hard?"

"Yeah, my brother gets hard when he touches it. It gets bigger. I've seen it. Does yours?"

Seth didn't know how to answer. Bill leaned forward, grabbing at him. Seth drew back, the faucet digging into his back. Bill yanked at him and Seth did nothing. He didn't know what to do, locked in his own head, he almost didn't react when Bill's dad opened the door and drug Bill out by his arm and hair. Seth turned and stared through the doorway. His dad had pulled Bill into the hallway and Seth could see shadows stretch out over the wall. Bill's dad screamed.

"We don't do that in this house! You hear me?!" And two huge strikes rang out. Open handed and sharp. Bill yelped.

"Please! It hurts!"

His dad's shadow rose and stiffened.

"Hurts? It's supposed to hurt you little pervert." Two more strikes.

"Always hanging on your mom! I know what's happening here!" Two more strikes. Each strike caused a ripple to shiver across the surface of the water. Then silence. Heavy footsteps walked back out to the front of the trailer and the door slammed. The muffled sounds of his father screaming outside leaked in through the bathroom window. Then the sound of Bill softly crying. Followed by slow, heavy footsteps back to the doorway. Bill's head and hand dipped into view, but not much more. Without making eye contact he said: "I think you should go."

Seth walked back to his trailer, water still dripping from his hair. He quietly sat on his stoop. The lights were still on and he didn't want to explain what had happened to his mother. Not tonight, or ever. So he waited. After a while he walked to the back of the trailer. Under the cover of darkness he began pulling on himself in the hopes that something would happen.

BLOWJOB HOUSE

Vicky had the honor of living in *Blowjob House*. The boys would sit on the hill by the community pool and watch as teenage boys would go knocking. They'd whisper to each other about what they thought was about to happen, needling each other with their elbows when the teenage boys made it inside. They were too young to really know what was going on at first. That's until the teenage boys all started talking.

They'd see the boys watching at a distance and would confidently saunter over to brag about what had just happened. One time Jimmy told them that it was his tenth time. They couldn't imagine it. Ten Blowjobs?

"Yeah, I'll let her suck me off. She likes it. But I don't fuck sluts. I'm not looking to catch something."

He'd hawk something up from his throat before

lighting a cigarette.

"See ya' round."

The boys all formed crushes on her from a distance. They would go home and fantasize about what the inside of her house must be like. And imagine themselves with her to the extent that they could. Mostly placing themselves in sex scenes from movies they secretly watched while their parents were sleeping. Those sections of the VHS worn out well before the rest of the tape. The fantasies amounted to little more than them laying on top of each other, breathing into each other's faces.

Vicky wasn't past fourteen when the rumors started. She'd gone on a date with Jimmy for the fourth of July. His dad drove them to a lake where the city was shooting off fireworks. He let Jimmy and Vicky lay in the bed of the truck for privacy. At first they tried to have a conversation but the wind was too loud and they spent most of the drive repeating their words getting closer and closer until they kissed. The wind whipped through her hair, twisting it into knots she knew she'd spend the entire night brushing out.

During the fireworks Jimmy's dad wandered off and spoke to other parents. Jimmy and Vicky made out in the bed of the truck with the fireworks bursting overhead. After some pushing Jimmy managed to get his hand down her shorts. Whatever he was doing didn't feel good, but all of this was new for Vicky and she didn't want to ruin the moment. This is how it was supposed to happen. Jimmy stopped talking to her after that night but told everyone that they had had sex.

In the evenings she walked past the swingset on her

way to the dumpster, trash bag in hand. All the boys
would stop what they were doing and watch. She could
feel their eyes and never turned to meet them. One day
a stringy teenager named Jake hopped off a swing and
walked up to the fence.

"Hey!"

She kept walking without turning.

"Vicky!"

She stopped and looked back. Jake had pulled himself
out of his swimming trunks and was thrusting through a
link in the fence.

"You want some more?"

Vicky walked up to the fence. Jake stared at her
through the links.

"Yeah? You want it slut?"

She wrapped her hand around him and yanked him
toward her. He let out screams. She grinded him against
the fence, catching his skin. She looked past him at the
boys without letting go.

"I don't do the things they say I do! Stop lying about
me!"

She let him go. He tried to spit at her but the thick
wad of spit got caught on the fence. He rolled himself
around in his hands assessing the damage. There was
blood, but not a lot of it. He zipped himself up and left
without a word.

The rumors never really stopped. Even after she died.
The moms in the neighborhood spent all day sunbathing.
The skin on their chests already cracked and bunching like
leather at the top of their breasts. They'd say: "Oh that
girl. She was asking for it. Going with all those boys." Her

parents would get looks that came from under green sun visors as they walked by. Half Judgment. Half Sympathy. Finally, about two years later, they moved away.

"I heard they got a divorce."

"I can understand why."

People would comment on how privileged they were. How they didn't belong there and would bring up the fact that Blowjob House was a doublewide. They'd cackle and say I wonder if they split it in half during the divorce.

PISSING CONTEST

There was a pond, not too far from the trailer park. The boys would walk up to it on the weekends, past the fancy development where they would trick-or-treat every year. They'd come back with pumpkin heads full of king size Snickers and whole bags of gummies. The boys spent all of their time together. Their group had slowly grown over the course of a year and now included Bill, Seth, Andrew, Paul and Chris.

The pond was narrow, and someone had spread hundreds of pounds of sand to create a small beach. But whenever it rained the water would rise and drag more and more sand right to the bottom of the pond. So once or twice a year it would be replenished. You'd hear the dump truck backing carefully up to the pond and dumping its load. Leaving it for the property owner to spread with a thick toothed aluminum rake.

The beach had been made so that people could lay out in the sun. But more often than not the couple alligators that lived in the pond would be out, sunning themselves and the people who lived around there would be too scared to leave their homes. When the boys came to the pond they looked forward to seeing the alligators. They would throw rocks at them and if they began to chase, would run from them like a game of tag, leaping over the black aluminum fence for safety. They're lazy animals. Most of the time they would go right on laying there, hissing at your back. But when they chased one of the boys it was always a thrill. The other boys would hang over the fence screaming "Run! Run!" or "Serpentine pattern!" like they were taught by their teachers in school.

Most middle schools ran safety classes about local wildlife. They would bring in a mustached man from the park services to speak to whole grades of children huddled on the library floor. He'd pace back and forth making strategic eye contact with each kid. It'd often start with him holding up a rubber Coral Snake. He'd tell them that it's easy to tell if the snake they were looking at was a Coral Snake or if they were another species that looked just like it. He'd raise his knobby finger to the rubber snake and say: "Red touch black, you're safe jake. Red touch yellow, you're a dead fellow." Then he'd nod and encourage the kids to say it with him. The whole room would repeat the phrase together in unison until he was satisfied. He'd tell them to always turn on the light if they went to the bathroom at night, because of the risk that a snake had swam up through the pipes and was now waiting for them in the toilet bowl. He'd pause for effect before changing direction and making eye contact with another kid.

"Never jump right into a pool. Walk slowly up to the edge and look down. Look at every corner of the pool to make sure that no alligators are wading on the bottom."

He'd clear his throat. Tell them to always check under their cars if they hear hissing. Never assume it's a tire going flat. He'd say: "They're incredibly fast in water and just as fast on land. You need to run in a serpentine pattern." This is what the boys would mimic. Half-serious, half-joking.

After pressing their luck long enough they'd usually head to Andrews and drink from the hose in the backyard. Sometimes they would pour it over their heads, soaking their clothes. And then let the sun dry them off before they'd head home.

At the back end of the park there were two enormous storm ditches that dropped at a 45 degree angle on all sides to a flat sandy bottom. When the boys were young they'd dig holes while their parents sat in lawn chairs at the top of the incline closest to the trailers. The parents would get sun burnt drinking tall boys and arguing about gossip. The park manager had allowed them to dig those holes until one time when they hit a cable line. The entire park lost cable access for days. He had a line of people out the door ready to complain that he had ruined their day off. After that he fined any parent whose kid was caught digging in the ditch.

When they got older they would take their bikes to the rim and challenge each other to race down the hill and up the other side. Most of the kids were too afraid to do it themselves. They'd egg each other on. Talking shit until one of them would cave and take the plunge. Usually they could make it. Other times they'd catch a wheel on a rock, and slide down on their backs, skinning their elbows while attempting to stop. The more timid riders would lock their legs and the bike pedals would gouge their shins at full force when they hit the bottom leaving them with blood running into their socks.

When hurricanes or heavy rains came in, the ditches would fill to the brim with water. A thin layer of grime and trash would float on the surface. It was a stagnant pool that could hang around for months and was a perfect mosquito breeding ground. The boys would take breaks from riding their bikes, walk over to the storm ditch and all pee together. They would see who could get the highest arch, whoever took the longest would get a half-hearted shove and almost fall in the murky water. When the ditches filled with water, as a precaution, the county would bring around fogger trucks to gas the park. When this happened, there was a 6pm curfew to protect people from the poison but that didn't keep them in their trailers. The moment the air thinned out, everyone would be back out on their cinder block stoops smoking and drinking.

The water drained into the ditches through four foot wide storm pipes. Huge concrete pipes with no bars on the front to keep people out. The older kids would makeout or smoke cigarette butts in the storm drains. The boys would dare each other to go in and crawl as far as they could without a flashlight. When they looked down the barrel of the drain at noon they could see a spot light shining through the top. This light was coming from a large drain that sat in the center of the street. They'd stand over the drain, heads dropped, trying to spit through the holes without bending over.

Finally one day, Bill dared Seth to crawl into the tube all the way to the drain. So that they could see him from above to make sure he didn't chicken out. There was a lot of back and forth. Seth tried to throw the dare to someone else. He said Bill was too afraid to do it himself. But none of it mattered, Seth was the one who'd have to do it.

Before crawling into the tube he pulled his raglan over his head and folded it up. His mom had just bought him that shirt and he didn't want to get it dirty. He crawled into the pipe and looked back at the four boys watching him. Bill made a "shew" hand motion and Seth began making his way toward the light. The boys were uncommonly silent as they climbed up the side of the ditch and over to the drain. They looked down through the grate and awaited Seth's appearance. None of them spoke. Bill's winded breathing was amplified by the hollow below him.

Fed up with waiting, Andrew yelled: "Hey! You down there?!"

No answer.

"C'mon dude! Did you chicken out?!"

Finally Seth's voice echoed out of the tube. "I'm coming! Jeez!"

His voice sounded close. Closer than the other boys thought he'd be. Chris had been watching the end of the ditch out of the side of his eye the whole time, expecting him to appear over the ridge, beaten by the challenge. Then, into the light of the drain, came Seth covered in brown muck. All of the boys cheered for him.

Seth looked up at them, shielding his eyes from the sun.

"Alright guys, can I come out?"

Then, a deep hiss came from the darkness of the pipe. Followed by a low guttural groan. The other boys heard it too.

"What was that?", one of them said.

They all knew what it was. Seth began backing down the tube slowly. Tucking his whole body. He was shaking and had to spread his arms out at his side to steady himself. The whole time he was trying to convince himself that what he'd heard was just in his head. That the other boys had psyched him out so much that he was hearing things. Then he heard something lurch forward. Something big. Seth turned and ran for the light.

The other boys rushed down the hill and back to the pipe.

"He's fucking dead!" Bill wheezed.

"Shut up!" Andrew called back.

Seth heard the sounds coming closer. There was nowhere to run but straight forward. No serpentine pattern. No way to move any faster. The ankle deep muck sucking his feet down with each step.

Seth burst from the mouth of the pipe where the boys were already waiting. He tumbled to the ground and quickly got back on his feet. They all stared down the pipe, unable to move, waiting for something to appear.

LACES

It was a well known fact that the trailer park was home to three sex offenders. All of them were required to go door to door and inform everyone of their status and where they lived. Their trailers were evenly spread throughout the park. No one was sure if this was strategic or not. From the time he had moved to the park, Seth had been warned about them by his mom. To never go near them. If he rode his bike past one of their trailers, give it a wide berth. Don't look at them. Never make eye contact. That's how they get you. This seemed crazy to him. It sounded more like she was describing monsters than people. He'd bombard her with confused questions but she never seemed to have a straight answer. She always talked around what they had done or how she knew they were bad.

Because of the evasiveness, their conversations

escalated the older he got. After a fight with her, mostly centering around his dad, Seth left the trailer in a huff. He pumped his bike petals as fast as they would take him, cutting through yards and past the playground. He was convinced that his mom just hated men. He thought it was unfair. He was convinced that she was hiding the truth from him. About his dad. About the men she would see once and then never see again. He didn't trust her. He didn't trust a word she said.

Something crossed his mind. A way to prove her wrong. He cut left down one of the streets that wasn't paved, just past the junk heap. Coming up on Sam's house he thought about the feeling of satisfaction coming his way. Knowing he proved his mom wrong.

Sam was the last sex offender to move in. He'd only lived there about six months and hadn't spoken to anyone since the initial door to door introductions. This made people suspicious. He could feel this, but didn't know what else to do. He knew if he approached them that people would make uncomfortable small-talk before excusing themselves from his presence. It had happened so many times before that he couldn't bring himself to try again.

Sam was crouched in his driveway next to his cinder block stoop. He'd built a small rock garden using a dozen bags of craggy white rocks and much of his time was focused on keeping them looking good. When he smoked he never flicked his ashes into them. Now he was on his haunches picking out small dead leaves that blew in from the neighbor's tree. They would get caught between rocks, and if Sam got lazy about picking them out they would accumulate and blanket the whole area. So one by one he'd pluck them from between the stones and set them into an empty Folgers can. In the middle of the night, he'd walk the Folgers can up to the dumpster to pour them out to avoid them blowing right back into the rock garden.

When Seth pulled up to the edge of his driveway, Sam was shocked. No kid had ever done this before. They rarely rode their bikes past his trailer at all. In fact, there was a groove being slowly worked into the grass a few houses over from kids cutting around his trailer entirely. Sam stood up.

"Can I help you."

Seth just stared at Sam.

"You really shouldn't be here. You could get me in trouble."

Nothing. But Seth couldn't look away.

"Go on!"

Sam leaned down and plucked a rock from the garden and pelted it at Seth.

"Get! Go on!"

Seth flinched, dodging the stone. He took off. There was a sinking feeling in his stomach. Something about the way Sam had looked at him. Seth had searched his eyes for goodness and hadn't felt any. Maybe his mom was right after all. On his way back home, his shoelace got caught in his petals and he crashed on the side of the road, skinning his knee. Once he freed himself he walked his bike home, limping the whole way. His bloody knee ended up being good cover. She didn't ask him where he'd gone or what he'd done. She assumed he was just tear-assing around, pouting. He was told to go wash his knee off. The scrape wasn't deep but had a wide spread and needed two big bandages to be covered completely. Before sticking the bandages in place, his mom blew on the knee. It was something he'd begun rejecting since he'd turned ten. Feeling like he was too old for certain things that made him feel like a little kid. But tonight was different. He enjoyed the familiarity and it made him feel safe.

<>

A week later Sam was jumped by a group of teenagers on one of his midnight garbage runs. He went into the hospital with a broken nose and two cracked ribs. They had filled tube socks with sand at the playground and tied off the open ends. After cornering him, they bludgeoned him with the socks, making sure to focus on his face. When the socks connected, the fabric spread just enough to let some sand through. The sand caked up in his eyes and had to be flushed out when he arrived in the emergency room. He wanted to press charges but the police never got back to him. Everyone assumed it was Jake and his friends, but no one cared enough to gossip.

BRUISED PALM

When I was maybe ten, a pipe burst in our trailer. Maybe I was eleven. It happened at night and the water only took seconds to rush out of the closet-sized bathroom and into the hallway. My mom leapt up and ran to the bathroom. I just remember her screaming. Not even making words. Just screaming. When I looked around the corner, she was on her knees, hand clasped around the pipe behind the toilet. Her palm up against the break in the pipe, attempting to hold the water in. The pressure made the water squeal as it misted through her fingers.

When she turned and saw me there she screamed "Turn the water off!". I didn't know how. I didn't know what she was talking about. She jerked her head towards the front of the trailer, "There! Up there! In front there's a box." I realized I knew what she meant and sprinted out the door and to the box. It was made of heavy duty plastic and stuck out of the ground about five feet from our trailer. When I opened the lid, I felt the dread fill me. I looked down into the box and all I saw was a hole in the ground. I didn't even know what I was looking for but there was nothing there to help.

I reluctantly walked back into the trailer. Afraid to tell her. When I did, she kept screaming "I can't hold this! I can't hold this!" She kicked at the wall next to her and dropped her head. She let go of the pipe and the sound of the water changed. It became a soft murmur. Her chin was at her chest and the trailer was still. She rose to her feet and shoved me out of the way as she passed. When I walked outside I saw her standing over the box. Her head was slumped, arms at her side. Looking back, I don't know why she thought there was anything in there that could help.

She turned and began walking up to her street. Her clothes were soaking wet and she left footprints on the street behind her. When she came back, Joe was with her. He had a tool case in his hand and was rubbing the sleep from his eyes. Joe was the person my mom called on any time there was a problem that required a "man's touch", in her words. He was some kind of handyman. More often than not, when we passed his trailer he was outside smoothing bondo into dents on his car. He'd sit outside shirtless all day. Burning in the sun. Paddle in hand. Running water over the bondo and nodding at everyone who passed.

When he walked into the trailer I remember hearing the carpet squish under his feet and him shouting "Holy

Cow". He never cursed. I remember that. The moment he entered the bathroom, the sound of the water disappeared. He peaked around the corner and said "Why didn't you turn the water off?". My mom stood there, arms crossed, saying nothing. He gestured to the toilet. "There's a knob on the back to cut the water. You just turn it and the water will stop. Didn't you know that?"

My mom blew up. She exploded about all of the things wrong in her life and how he was a problem too. About how she shouldn't have to know things like that and how she wasn't stupid for not knowing. Anything she felt insecure about lacking was always something a man should know. And that there should be a man around but there isn't.

Something happened mid-tirade that I wasn't expecting. Joe, this middle-aged hyper-masculine man, started weeping and asking her to stop. But she didn't. There was always a rage in her that compelled her to double down on cruelty.

I don't remember when, but I left the room at some point and buried myself under my blanket. The walls were thin enough that even after she calmed down and they moved to the living room I could still hear every word that was said. Joe explained to her how he'd been molested as a kid and now he couldn't deal with yelling anymore. And how she's not allowed to speak to him like that, especially when he comes over to help. I just remember my mom saying "I didn't know that." defensively and refusing to apologize.

The next day we opened up both doors and set boxed fans in front of them. The soaked wooden panels moaned under our feet. As they dried, they curled to points, almost ripping holes in the carpet in some places. The floor was never the same and you could hear every step taken from anywhere inside. The following weeks I caught my mom staring at her bruised palm. One time she started slamming it on the counter, only stopping when she caught me looking. She said, "Joe's dangerous. We're not going to see him anymore." When I asked why she said: "People who have been raped, rape. It gets inside them and they can't help it... If they were smart they'd lock them all up when it happens. Save us a lot of trouble... There's no fixing him now. He's not a man anymore."

THE JOGGER

She always ran her laps around the trailer park at dawn. No one was out and it was the one time she felt like she wasn't being watched. What she didn't know is that she was part of Bill's morning routine. He was always up early, before his parents, and would throw on music videos with the volume turned down while he ate cold cereal. He would stand at the big window in the front of the trailer, bowl in hand, waiting for her pass by. Bill had never seen an anorexic woman before. He hadn't even heard that word before his mom had said it to him. She snuck up behind him that morning, taking care to make every movement as steady as possible. Her chin hovered over his shoulder unnoticed until the runner went by and then out came her scream.

"Don't look at her", she snapped in his ear, startling

him. "She's anorexic. She's sick. Don't look at her."

She corralled him to her side, pressing her face through the curtains, to the glass. He felt her growing mad. He stared up at her silhouette against the window. She looked like an enormous bug.

"Look at her. This is why men don't respect women anymore." She turned back. "Women like me. She's the reason why men like your father don't look at women like me anymore." Bill couldn't understand why his mom was so angry if she was sick. If she was sick, how was it her fault? He wanted to know more but knew he couldn't ask. He looked up into her angry eyes and knew his only choice was to nod his head.

From then on he became fascinated by the jogger. He started eating his breakfast outside every morning so he could watch her without his mom catching him. It seemed like every time he saw her she had lost even more weight. He didn't understand what anorexia was but he understood that it had to be something bad. There was a pang of excitement when she would round the curve. He shoveled cereal into his mouth and chewed, letting his bites match the rhythm of her steps.

He never got the chance to speak to her, until the following Halloween. It was the same year someone dressed up in a KKK outfit and no one could tell if it was a joke or for real. He showed up at the neighborhood halloween party. The one that was held in the small clubhouse every year. No one asked him to leave but everyone stood silent and awkwardly hoping he'd go. After a while he caught the hint and left. Some teens jumped him by the mailboxes before he could get home. They broke his jaw in two places and he spent the rest of winter with his jaw wired shut. This let everyone know who was under that hood.

Bill was walking to Andrew's to meet up before trick or treating. Andrew had already gone out at the beginning of the night. He had just gotten back to change his costume from Batman to a ninja. He did this every year. The second costume was always something thrown together at the last second so that he could get double the candy. To his surprise, only one person had ever recognized him. It was an older woman who had commented that another boy that night had the same exact shoes. Then it clicked in her mind. She shouted "You little rat!" at him, as he was already running away.

Bill and Andrew walked side-by-side with their heads hanging, looking down into their buckets. They took note of how much candy they'd gotten so far that night and tried to remember which houses gave them the disappointing candies like Bit-o'honey. Bill lifted his head and stopped walking. Andrew did the same, looking at Bill's face.

"What's wrong?"

Bill kept his eyes locked ahead of him. Andrew turned to see what he was looking at. It was the jogger. She was stretching against a transformer on the corner of their street. Bent over with her hands wrapped around her foot, she let out a long slow breath. Bill couldn't look away from her. Her thigh was the same size as her forearm. The strings of her muscles were more defined at her elbows and knees. He felt like he could see through her skin in some places. Andrew was just as horrified. This is the first time he'd ever seen her himself. Bill had told him about her before but Andrew had assumed he was kidding. She turned to them and flashed a smile. Her gums were inflamed and pulled back high on her teeth. One of Bill's feet began to float backward and he had to stop himself from running.

"You guys having fun?" She pointed to their candy buckets. "Isn't Halloween the best?!" she said with mock-excitement.

Bill had imagined this moment for so long but he found himself speechless now that he was face to face with her. She was talking to him. What did he want to say?

Finally he blurted out: "My mom says you're anorexic." The smile slowly dropped from her face. "Are you okay? Are you sick?" Bill wished he hadn't said it. But he couldn't take it back now. Her brow rose and wrinkled in anger. Her eyes grew thin.

"Hey fuck you kid. Tell your mother that's none of her fucking business." She began running away. "Little dirtbag."

They watched her as she disappeared down the street.

"C'mon let's go." Andrew said.

Bill didn't budge. Andrew saw the anger on his face and wasn't sure what had just happened. Bill stomped back in the direction they came. Andrew followed.

"Bill, where are we going?"

Bill said nothing. When they came up to Bill's house Andrew waited in the street. Andrew didn't like going into his house. It always gave him a bad feeling. Bill took forever. Andrew kicked at the chipping spray paint on the driveway, considering whether or not he should leave. He could still make one more round without Bill if he hurried.

Finally, Bill reemerged with toothpaste and toilet paper in hand.

"C'mon." He said, hiding the items in his candy bucket.

They walked to her trailer and stepped out of the light and into the shadows. Bill watched the street, waiting for her to finish her run. Until a light flicked on inside. She'd beaten them back. "C'mon we should go." Andrew said, pulling at Bill's sleeve.

Bill yanked is arm away.

"No! You heard what she said to us."

Andrew shrugged at him.

"I don't even know what happened."

Bill ignored Andrew, waiting for the light inside of the trailer to go out. When the window went dark he crept up and tossed the toilet paper roll over her trailer.

"Quick go grab it and throw it back!"

Andrew watched him confused.

"Why are you doing this?"

Bill shuffled to the other side of the trailer to grab the toilet paper and throw it back.

"Aren't you going to help me?!"

The roll came sailing back over and landed at Andrew's feet. Bill ran back around, winded. Andrew stepped back from the toilet paper roll. Bill shook his head in disappointment. He reached into his candy bucket and pulled out the toothpaste. He uncapped the tube and began running it along her vinyl siding. His older half-brother had told him it'd eat through the paint and he'd always wanted to know if that was true. Andrew knocked the tube out of his hand before he could get more than two feet.

"What'd you do that for?"

Andrew leaned in.

"C'mon, we're going to get in trouble."

Bill looked betrayed.

"She hates my mom. She wants her to feel bad! Didn't you see her?"

The light in the trailer sprang back on and the boys sprinted away, weaving between trailers to avoid being seen. Once they were back on the street they didn't speak for a long time. Just as they were approaching Andrew's trailer, Bill grabbed Andrew by the arm and wrestled him to the ground. He clamped down with both of his big palms and dragged them in different directions. Andrew screamed in pain.

"The next time I tell you to do something, you do it faggot! I thought you were my friend." Bill let him go and stood back up. Andrew, locked on Bill with fire in his eyes. He rose and tackled Bill into the street, his head bouncing off the concrete. Andrew punched at the sides of his head, not quite sure what he was doing. Bill let out cries through his hands. The door on the trailer behind them swung open and an older man screamed "Hey! You get out of here!"

The fight was over. The boys shared glances and saw tears coming out of each other's eyes. They got back up without words and headed to their own trailers, alone.

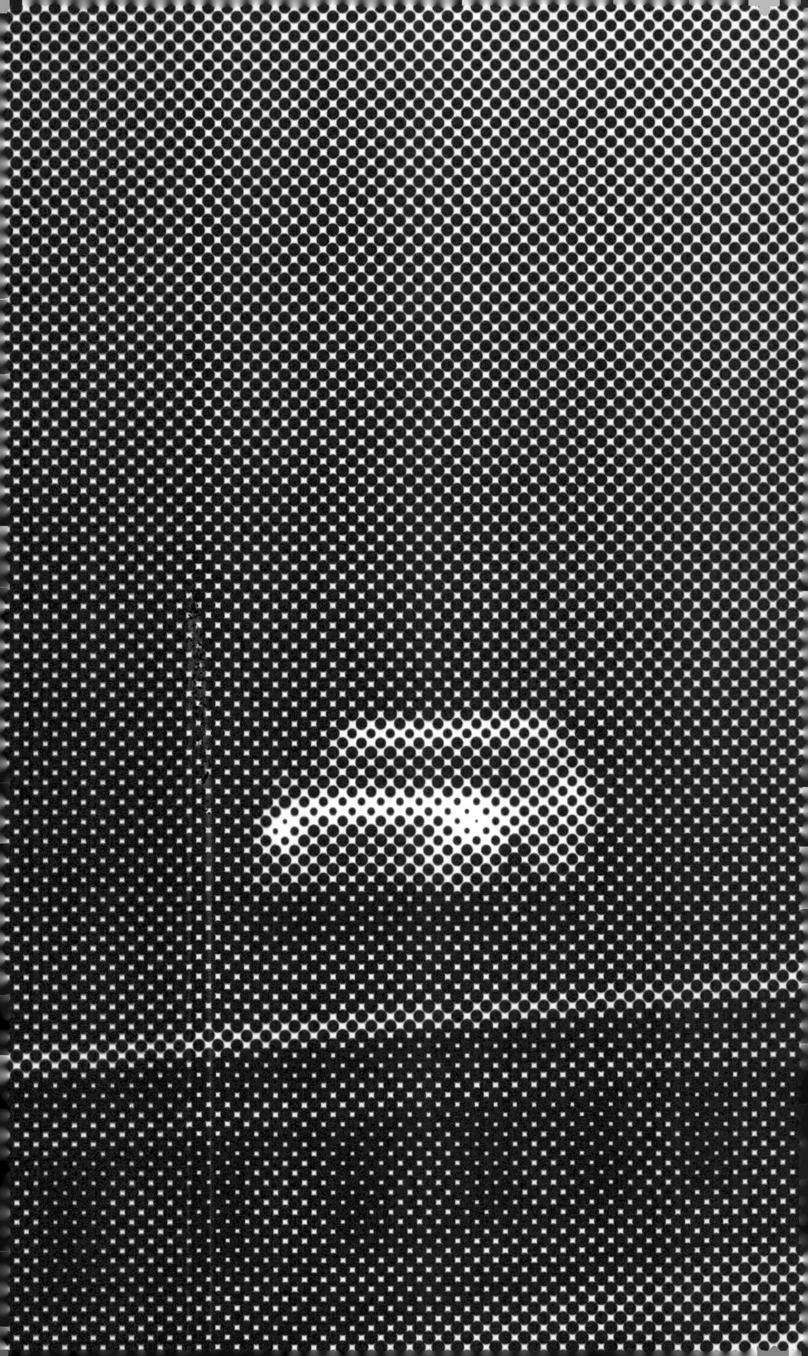

EVACUA-
TION

All of the women were putting x's on the windows with masking tape. This is what the weathermen suggested if you couldn't afford to board them up. It didn't make much sense to Seth. If something flew through the window it was going to break either way. He watched his mom move from one window to the next, peeling off large strips of tape and ripping them off with her teeth. He pictured them staying in the trailer through the storm. A branch flying through the window and impaling her. All of the muscles in his body tensed at this thought.

Another hurricane was bearing down on Florida and their county was told to evacuate. When this happened, most families in the park would pack up what they could and head to the largest high school in the district. Some families would stay behind and ride it out. Figuring if their trailer blew away what else did they have to lose. Might as well go with it.

Seth was let out of school early that day. A pitch black cloud shelf came rolling in just after second period. The sky went from a cloud free bright blue to total darkness before noon. The teacher did her best to keep the class focused but the kids couldn't help stare outside. It looked like it could have been midnight out there. Lightning jumped from cloud to cloud.

The buses rushed the students home. By the time Seth got off the bus the rain was coming in horizontally. Many of the kids were dropped off to empty houses. They would have to wait in their rooms, walls rattling, waiting to see what would happen.

After Seth's mom had gotten divorced she vowed to never let anything bad happen to him and had mostly kept to that promise. When he walked in the door he tripped over a paper grocery bag filled with his clothes. A ziplock bag sat on top with toothbrushes, toothpaste, and other essentials. His mom was raiding the pantry. Shoving boxed cereal, crackers, chips and cans of coke into another grocery bag. She turned to him. "Get your coat on. We have to go." Seth looked toward his room.

"But what about all my stuff?"

"I've got you packed up right there."

Seth looked at the paper grocery bag he'd tripped over. "That's it?"

"Yes, get your coat on now!"

"But what about my toys? My video games?"

She let out a sigh. "We can't take everything. I'm sorry." And just like that, the argument was over. He knew that tone. And he knew to give up.

This wasn't the first time his mom had condensed her life down to a few bags. She'd lived in Florida her entire life and she knew not to get too attached to anything. She didn't get romantic about property. Sooner or later it would get washed away or you would get rid of it yourself, no matter how much you think you care about it in the beginning.

The windshield wipers whipped back and forth as they made their way down the road. Seth sat in the passenger seat and couldn't see more than five feet in front of the car. He turned to his mom, examining her face for signs that everything would be alright. The windshield kept fogging and every few minutes she would run her palm across the glass, letting off squeaks. Four by fours swerved past her, letting out a horn squeal that kept ringing out well after they'd disappeared into the rain ahead.

At the high school people amassed in the large cafeteria. People brought cots and air mattresses. They brought in bags of McDonalds, who were riding out the entire storm. Old women with nasal cannulas looped around their ears sat next to stacks of oxygen tanks, hoping that they had enough oxygen to last the coming days. Some of them turned their intake down to half. Expecting to spend the next three days out of breath, but with any luck, alive.

Teenagers snuck off to closets and classrooms once it got dark. A young couple in the science wing made out on one of the teacher's desks. The boy was sure she'd finally go all the way with him, until she accidentally knocked the lamp from the desk, shattering its green glass shade. They fled the room soon after. Other teenagers huddled in stairwells smoking weed, talking abstractly about losing everything in the storm, stopping just shy of acknowledging that it would happen to them.

Seth noticed that a young hispanic couple and their three children were tucked into a corner of the cafeteria, passively watching as their youngest son played Nintendo. He stared at them for a long time. Later that night when Seth's mom spooned with him on a pile of pillows in one of the many hallways, he remained stiff.

"Is everything alright?" she asked.

He pulled away.

"You lied. There are kids in there with video games, and toys and everything."

A long sigh and then: "Seth, we couldn't bring it all."

"You lied."

"I lied?..... Okay maybe I did." She cupped her face in her hands. "I just get so tired sometimes..." She trailed off. Before long she was asleep.

The power died sometime around 2am and the hum of the school's generator could be heard in the distance from that point on. The room grew wet. The air was thick with the smell of everyone breathing and taking up space. Seth never fell asleep. He couldn't stop thinking about the Nintendo next door and how unfair it was. Even now, when the power was out and everyone was depending on that generator. Sometime after college, he'd divulge this story to a friend in a moment of drunken weakness. He'd liken the feeling to a time he missed the majority of a concert because he spent the whole show sitting in a bathroom stall, with his phone in his hands, waiting for a text from a girl who never showed up. His half-empty Pabst Blue can tenuously resting on a toilet paper dispenser next to him.

He rose up and snuck into the cafeteria room. He stepped between all of the sleeping people lying on the ground. Doing his best not to rouse them. The boy's hands were still wrapped around the controller as he slept. The mario menu looped on the muted tv. Seth pressed the power button and the image of the menu turned to white noise. He pulled the cartridge from the console, intent on breaking it. When he rose up with the game in his hands a feeling came over him. He felt like he was being watched. He turned and saw one of the old women on oxygen. Her breathing was heavy as she stared him down. She didn't say anything. Just shook her head slowly. Her eyes sank to the game in his hands. Then back up to his eyes. Seth rested the game on the floor and headed back to the hallway where his mom was still sleeping. He curled up against her chest and tucked his knees to his own.

Seth and his mom left the shelter three days later. When they got back home, they found that the car port had blown off their trailer, dragging a section of gutter with it. The gutter hung at the side of the house, swaying in the wind. The car port had blown out of the trailer park and down the street, finally coming to a stop when it busted through the bay window of a much nicer house, just under a mile away. His mom had discovered this after driving around, hoping it could be salvaged. She sat in her parked car and watched the owner of the home, an old balding man, try and pry the metal from his window. She wanted to get out and help, but the thought that she may be found liable for damages kept her from moving. No insurance company ever contacted her. She never replaced the car port or the gutter. When it rained the water would fall in thick streams and erode huge holes in the dirt around the house. That winter marble-sized hail came down and left two spiderweb cracks in the windshield of her car, parked in the open driveway.

STEALING ORANGES

There were twin sisters who always wore their hair in ponytails. They had been raised Baptist at first but their parents had chosen to convert to Jehovah's Witness just after they turned seven. This gave the girls an elevated sense of self-worth that the other puberty stricken kids had a deficit of. On hot summer days they would walk around the trailer park and quickly steal the oranges from the few spindly trees people had planted behind their trailers. They would walk door to door with the stolen oranges and proselytize, claiming that they were selling the oranges for a Kingdom Hall fundraiser.

Most people didn't buy it. They would look down at these two girls, arms cradling the freehanded oranges, and just shake their heads No. Amia, the younger one by five minutes, took this personally. One time she even dropped the oranges to her feet and began pelting the side of the trailer with them until the owner came back out and chased them to the corner.

Vicky hated the twins. They would knock on her door every weekend and ask her to play. In their minds, play actually meant getting her to the playground. There they would first bring up how scary hell must be. They'd tell her she was going to hell unless she joined their Kingdom Hall. All it took was a handful of debates before Vicky was done with them. But they never took the hint.

When Vicky's dad was working extra hours, her and her mom would go on grocery runs. They had the whole day to kill and her mom would stand patiently as Vicky thumbed through every magazine on the rack. Her mom would pass the time by reading the backs of discount horror and romance novels on the nearby stand.

When they got back to the trailer park her mom would drive up to the mailboxes and have Vicky run to grab the mail. Some days Vicky would ask her mom to time her to see how fast she could do it. Her mom would look down at the underside of her wrist, imagining a watch there, and after a beat shout "Go!" Vicky would run as fast as she could. Her flip flops snapping at her heels. "One Mississippi! Two Mississippi!" Her mom would call after her. She'd sink the key into the lock and yank the mail from inside. There was a slope up to the mailboxes and when she came running back down it she would pick up extra speed and leap into the passenger seat. "How did I do?" Her mom would look up from her imaginary watch and say: "You did great". She never gave her an actual time.

Vicky had forgotten how she first convinced her mom

to let her do it, but on days her dad wasn't home she'd hang on the back of the car from the mailboxes to their trailer. Her mom drove a navy blue Ford Escort hatchback. Vicky would stand on the back bumper and hold onto the roof rack like it was a handle. Her mom would drive slowly down the road, hugging the brakes as she went over the speed bumps. On days Vicky was feeling brave she would tighten her grip and let her feet dangle from the back of the car. She would feel like she was floating. She'd close her eyes and yell "Yahoo!" All the while her mom would watch her through the rear view mirror, ensuring she was safe.

When they arrived home her mom would hold her by the shoulders and crouch down to speak to her.

"This is our secret."

"Our secret" Vicky would repeat after her.

"We're never telling daddy, alright."

Vicky would nod in agreement.

GROUP ACTIVITY

As the boys hit puberty, Bill became the hookup for porn. His dad had so many magazine subscriptions he couldn't keep track of them and this made it easy for Bill to snag one here and there, assuming his father wouldn't notice or just chalk it up to the issue getting lost in the mail. Bill was always surprised by his mother's calm surrounding the magazines.

They were a pile family. Every particle board end table was covered in piles to the point that the wood would bow under the weight. And to help reinforce it, a pile would be made underneath. The issues of Cherry, Juggs, Easy Rider and a half dozen others would be left out in the open surrounded by mugs and dishes covered in stuck-on food. And the policing of the material wouldn't go past his mom reminding him every month or so that those were his fathers, and they were for grown ups.

The other boys were blindsided by this openness and if an issue happened to be resting on the top of the stack they would struggle not to stare at the cover out of the side of their eyes. They would focus on the tv unblinkingly, imagining drops of sweat rolling down their temples, hoping to whip their eyes over at an opportune moment. Then devote that image to memory, planting it as deeply as possible for later use.

Things got easier, and more complicated, when Andrew's mom got transferred to second shift. The boys would all ride their bikes over and crowd into the trailer. It started with them all taking turns with the magazine in the bathroom, one at a time. As time went by they would start pairing, never looking at each other and always doing their business under the counter while staring down at the pre-agreed on page.

Just after Bill turned 12 his dad accidentally signed up for a video subscription service, and unable to cancel, VHSs would show up on a bi-weekly basis for the next 12 months. This was a game changer for the boys. His dad, still bitter about the money he felt he'd been scammed out of, never even opened the VHSs. He'd just stack them in one of the spare drawers in his dresser. Once a half dozen had built up, Bill slipped one from the stack and headed to Andrew's with the other boys. Andrew's house only had one VHS player. It was a small 14 inch tube Zenith combo that rested on the kitchen counter.

Bill inserted the tape with sweaty palms and the screen sparked to life. All of them stood frozen and would have fallen into a trance had they not been so aware of each other's presence. The woman on screen was a blonde with big curled bangs and perfect lipstick. She had on black french cut lingerie. The camera slowly zoomed back to reveal her dancing. Throwing her weight hip to hip. She brought her hands up to her head and tried to fluff her hair, stiff with hairspray. This went on for what seemed like forever. Then she began undoing the clips on the front of her top and two enormous fake breasts burst out. Seth reached to touch the image of her breast. The screen crackled with static electricity against his fingertips.

The sound of a zip and the boys saw Bill's shorts hit the floor. He looked back at them confused. "What? Are we going to do this?"

They looked between each other.

"I just don't want you to see me." One of them said.

"Yeah, I want to. I just don't..."

They were all on their backs. Lying on the floor with pillows turned on their sides between them. Bill took his shirt off before getting settled in. The other boys shot uncomfortable glances between them. The sounds their hands were making made them uncomfortable. Andrew grabbed the remote with his free hand and upped the volume. Filling the trailer with muzak and performative moans. The scene ended and another began, this time with a redhead. The boys kept going at themselves, making little progress. After a while they didn't even want to see the screen anymore, so they clamped their eyes shut.

Chris caught himself staring at Andrew, who was laying directly to his right. He noticed the way his hair fell on his face. The flare of his nostrils as his breaths shortened. Chris felt his neck craning over, able to see more and more of his torso as his chest rose and fell. His belly button and his slender hip bone. Chris yanked himself back in place when he felt Andrew's eyes open. The two silently shared a look. Chris didn't know what he would do. He was expecting him to yell out and tell the other boys about him looking. Make him a pariah. Andrew's head slowly turned away and his eyes locked back onto the tv.

Bill finished with a groan. He didn't want to get up or be seen by the others so he was left with the awkward burden of sitting in his mess until the others finished. He stared up at the ceiling, trying to block out the sound of the tv, that only moments ago had been so appealing. A wave of shame washed over him. For some reason a memory of breaking his toys popped into his head. His mom had found him, crushing his action figures with a rock. She grabbed his arm and threw him to the ground. Looming over him, she yelled: "Only bad kids break their toys! Only kids that grow up to be crazy break their toys!" He was back there with her again. Helpless. On his back.

The boys never went back to Andrews trailer after that. Something had changed. The boys found other ways to get their hands on porn and Bill never offered again. Over the following months, they hung out with Chris less and less. He'd have panic moments wondering if Andrew had said something. Maybe it was just them growing apart. Seth was spending more time with his cousin who had recently moved a mile away. Chris would spot him walking there from his mom's car as they drove by. He'd wave but Seth never seemed to see him.

CUL - DE - SAC

Danny was a thin man but he was getting a belly, and when it crossed his mind he would suck it in if he was in public. He was thirty-five and often asked himself how he ended up in this place. Loneliness followed him around and he didn't do much to try and shake it. He was an insecure man and felt bad for himself more than he should. He looked down on the other people in the trailer park. Whenever he got the chance, he'd explain to whoever would listen how he wasn't a redneck and didn't belong there. But everyone else? They were were rednecks. He'd walk by every trailer and list what was wrong with each one. Untamed ivy growing inside the vinyl siding. Rusty gutters. Dead patches of grass. He'd spot it all.

He didn't like speaking with anyone in the park and as a result he isolated himself even further. He waited until nightfall to walk his garbage bag up to the trash compactor. "Decompression Time" is what he would call it. He'd walk slowly, peeking into all of the illuminated windows as he passed. Cheap white curtains would almost always block his view.

He'd tried a video dating service earlier that year but never heard back from anyone. It was a struggle for him to write out a summation of himself. He sat in his kitchen for days jotting down half-sentences that he immediately crossed out. When he arrived at the studio to film his listing, he was in a flop sweat on account of wearing a suit he'd bought for an aunt's funeral. It was the only dressy clothing he had. His description of himself read like the opening statement to a deposition. Interests were alluded to but never outright stated. Every time he started a sentence with "um" or "well" he tensed up, knowing that they wouldn't be cut from the final product. Years later he would decry the dating service, claiming they never sent it out, just to ridicule him.

The trash bag landed in the compactor with a thud, blowing a cloud of trash smell in his face. He pulled the heavy door shut and headed back home. As he passed he spotted Vicky lingering at the playground, smoking cigarettes with a boy he didn't recognize. He gave a half wave to them out of habit but was relieved when they didn't respond.

Danny usually rushed home. But something was different about that night. He hadn't seen anyone else and wanted to linger in the warm air. He ambled in a serpentine pattern, gliding from one side of the road to the other. When he came to a speed bump he stopped and ran his foot over the rough plateau. He hadn't thought until now about how powerful the grinder must have been to take the top off of each asphalt mound.

For whatever reason, every street in the trailer park shared the same name. Making it hard to tell other residents where you lived. People would resort to categorical sentences like: "I live on the back street, the one past the playground, kind of down. There's a transformer. A palm tree a couple houses down." Everyone would nod politely, acting like they understood.

The center street had a small cul-de-sac at its center that only held five houses. Danny had never entered that cul-de-sac. He'd lived in the trailer park for more than five years and had spent the whole time avoiding the truth, saying that he'd be moving along any time now. He'd never explored. He never decorated his living room. He didn't even know about the junk heap in the back. Which might have been a solution to the flat tire sucking up the space in his shed.

He stood at the mouth of the cul-de-sac. All of the trailers were lit up and seemed much more cozy to him. They glowed yellow. The landscaping was immaculate. The cars in the driveways were newer. He put one foot in front of the other until he found himself in the center of the circle. One trailer caught his eye. Its curtains were wide open. He could see right into the living room. A woman was pacing the room, struggling to remove a barrette from her hair. He moved closer. The fast food polo she was wearing came over her head and a moment later her bra was off. She rubbed at the impressions left in her skin by the bra. Then raised her arms and stretched her back, jutting her breasts out carelessly.

Danny didn't feel his mouth go agape. She moved toward the window and grasped the drawstring on the mini-blinds, but stopped. She stared out the window. For a moment Danny went blank. He knew she wasn't just looking at her own reflection in the window. She was looking at him. They both stood frozen, staring into each other through the thin pane of glass. At that moment Danny realized how alone he'd become. He wished that she'd press herself against the glass, beckoning him in. That she'd feel the lust he did for her. Maybe if she met him they'd hit it off. Maybe she was here, waiting for him this entire time and he just didn't know it until now. She fumbled with the drawstring and the blinds boxed him out. Seconds later the window went dark. Danny wasn't sure what to expect. Maybe shouting, or sirens, but nothing happened. He quickly walked home.

The next day he didn't leave his trailer. He spent most of the day feeling equal parts guilty and electrified. It felt like something had rejogged him. But when he thought of the look on her face he came right back down to earth. The following night he left just after 10pm. He took the long way to the cul-de-sac. When he got there he saw that a fleece blanket was now hung up in the window. Likely nailed into the wall the following day. That's when he began having phantom sensations down the lower half of his legs, like bugs or rodents were crawling through his hair. He would become short of breath out of nowhere. And more than once he had an uncontrollable crying fit in a grocery aisle.

Weeks later a siege of caterpillars infested the trailer

park. They clung to every tree and covered them in nests that looked like fake halloween store cobwebs. Thousands were squashed in the road by passing cars and dried out in the sun. Children smashed them with plastic shovels and inspected their bright green insides with plastic magnifying glasses.. Danny's tree seemed to get the worst of it. In the back of his mind, he felt that maybe he had caused this. That this was his punishment and that everyone else knew it too.

BLE ACHED HAIR

Chris' dad worked construction. One summer his dad was offered a high paying job working at a resort being built in the upper part of the state. So Chris was passed off to his grandma for a few months until his dad could come home.

She also lived in a trailer park but it was a much nicer one. There was an electric gate at the entrance that would only open if you entered a four digit pin number. The park had a lot more trees. Spanish moss would hang from all of the branches and old timers would collect it in grocery bags and use it as kindling to start fires in the fall. There was a much larger pool. People would tell Chris that it was Olympic-sized but he wasn't sure what that meant.

Most of the time his grandma would sleep the days away and Chris would rollerblade around the neighborhood. The lonely elderly couples sitting in their screened porches would wave and ask him who he was staying with. The park's policy was that no one under fifty could be a resident but this went mostly ignored. Other grandchildren would end up there from time to time, but Chris would never seek them out. He liked his time alone. He spent days stealing books from the small clubhouse library and reading them under palm trees. Long days were spent in the pool allowing the sun to bleach his hair blonde. He'd float under the surface of the water and watch as the elderly couples did water exercises. Their loose skin bobbed through the water, brown as a roast chicken.

When his grandma was asleep in the living room he'd go through her bedroom, trying on her bras. He'd press himself up against a floor length mirror and vamp. When he pulled her nylons over his feet his budding leg hair would reach out through the fabric and stand out straight. Shame would wash over him and he would stuff the clothing back into her drawers, doing his best to return it to the way he had found it.

She was more or less a shut in and had trouble getting around. When they would go to the store once a week Chris would hold her hand to keep her steady. He'd slow down his steps to match her pace, grabbing items from the lower shelves that she had trouble reaching.

Dead skin would build up on the bottoms of her feet and he would use a dry pumice stone to sand it down, her feet elevated on a glider ottoman. At Chris' suggestion she bought pink nail polish with glitter. He would do her nails every few weeks. When the polish chipped he would use nail polish remover to take it off and apply a new coat.

She'd return the favor by cutting his hair. Her shaky hands would leave the layers uneven.

When Chris had to return home in August he put up a fight. He didn't want to go back to his old bedroom and old friends. He wanted to stay in that serene place he'd found, where his days were spent following a routine and someone depended on him.

FAKING SLEEP

Andrew's mom worked second shift. Her shift would start at 4pm and she'd get off around Midnight. Add in the bus ride and she'd make it home around 12:45am. She couldn't afford a babysitter so when Andrew turned ten she started leaving him at home alone. There was a hide-a-key hidden under their cinder block stoop. Every day he'd let himself in and make dinner. It usually consisted of boxed mac n' cheese, spaghetti or oatmeal. These were cheap, calorie heavy options that didn't require much prep. Andrew always found it strange that she didn't trust him with one of the dull knives in the drawer, but she was perfectly fine with him boiling a large pot of noodles on their gas range.

Around the time Andrew turned eleven or twelve the routine changed. He'd rush home, not taking time to linger with the other boys, get completely naked, and masturbate to a magazine he'd stolen from Bill. Usually opting for the same centerfold every day. The image was of a pair of women with curly brunette hair, breast implants and shaved public hair. They had their bodies intertwined, giving them the appearance of a two headed spider. He would notice something different every time he reached under the mattress and peeled the magazine open. The scars under their breasts, left untouched by the airbrush. Or the patch of razor burn on one of their upper thighs. He wasn't aware of it, but this is how fantasies break down. When you spend too much time lingering on the details, realism creeps in.

After he finished, he would pick up his old routine as usual. At a certain point he began ignoring his mother's pleas to not use the knives. He'd boil ramen and make it more filling by dicing up whatever vegetables were in the fridge. Usually carrots because you could buy them cheaply in bulk and they took forever to go bad. He'd lay belly down on the trailer floor slurping noodles, but would rarely do his homework. Instead, he'd be caught up in something on tv before his pencil hit the paper.

His mom had taken the second shift because it paid 10 cents more per hour, and that made a major difference. It messed with her sleep schedule. She would arrive home unable to keep her eyes open, but by the time she got cleaned up for bed she'd be wide awake.

She would lie in bed, eyes closed, hoping for sleep. In the back of her mind she thought maybe if she tried to read, or if she watched something it would calm her. Maybe help her fall asleep. But she never tried it out.

Second shift changed something about the way that she viewed her time off the clock. It was late. You don't watch tv this late, or listen to music or do anything. This was the time you were supposed to sleep. She thought it would be better to just stay put, pillow between her legs, eyes closed. Faking her way into sleep.

Andrew would always be in his bedroom, biding his time until he heard the sounds of her snoring. He was well suited to being up late. His body craved that schedule. When she first started second shift he would stay up late watching movies and drawing. And when his mom got home they would talk about their days. He was excited to see her and he felt himself miss her easily. But as he got older, he wanted to keep to himself more and more. When she would arrive home he'd feel a rush of anxiety pulse through him. He felt implicitly that he was being judged.

Her eyes had grown tired and her temper shorter. So to avoid conflict he found himself avoiding contact. Once he could tell she was asleep, he would sneak out to the living room and watch movies on mute. Or read a book by the tv light until his eyes couldn't focus anymore.

One afternoon, when he inevitably reached for the magazine, it wasn't there. He lifted his whole mattress and it was nowhere to be found. He felt his whole body grow warm with panic. He felt dread imagining the punishment when she arrived home. But this fear quickly subsided. This wasn't the first time something like this had happened. He'd had another magazine confiscated the prior summer without a word. This is how she parented. At random, Andrews' mom would do a sweep of his bedroom, like she was tossing a cell, and take anything she found inappropriate. No muss. No fuss. There was never any punishment. Andrew would sit in this discomfort. Knowing that his space had been violated and would wait for a punishment that wasn't coming. By this point they had hit a full-blown cold war and neither of them was going to risk bringing it to a head.

That night she arrived home later than usual. He had been sitting in the darkened living room watching tv when he heard her walking up the drive. He snapped the tv off and rushed to his room on his tip-toes. He closed his door behind him, flew into bed, wrapped himself in the blanket, clamping his eyes shut.

When she came in, she was usually quick to the bathroom and then to bed. But something was different tonight. He could feel her lingering at the door and she sounded like she was crying. Finally his door cracked open and in a phlegmy voice she said his name. He laid there motionless. He knew something was wrong but didn't want to hear what it was. *"I just want her to leave me alone."* He kept saying in his own head. She knew he was faking it. She could always tell when he was really asleep. Her mouth opened to say his name again but nothing came out. She closed the door. Andrew let out a long sigh and fell into a deep sleep in only moments.

She shuffled to her bed, circumventing that night's shower. She'd been let go. She didn't know what she was going to do. File employment the next morning, but what after that? Now that he hadn't answered her, the idea of not even telling him was rolling around in her head. It was late. And even though she had nowhere to be the next day, her body pulled her to the bed. She laid down, pillow between her legs, eyes closed, waiting for sleep.

DEAD LOT

Everyone was relieved when Joe moved away. He was the owner of a massive truck that had been put on a lift. It sat in his yard just off the street because it was too tall to fit under the carport. The alarm he installed was either too sensitive or too cheap. Whenever a car drove down the narrow street the alarm would echo for a quarter mile. On top of that, this would usually happen just after 2 a.m. when the bars let out. Joe was drunk asleep half the time so the alarm could ring for 20 minutes before he'd drag his ass out and turn the thing off. You could see him through your windows, stumbling to the driver's side door, hands over his ears. To get into the cab he'd have to use the front tire as a springboard, wedging his foot in between the big black grooves of rubber. Once the alarm was silenced, he'd walk back in and collapse face down on his bed, his feet staining the sheets black.

When Joe moved away a family from Trinidad moved in. Everyone said they came from Jamaica because they didn't know the difference. They painted over the gray aluminum siding with bright yellow paint and coated the trim in a deep brown. The kids took to calling the place Banana House. Their parents told them to never go in that trailer no matter what. There were suggestions of voodoo rituals and drugs that turned you into zombies. Most of the kids disregarded these claims, because they seemed to have better sense than most of their parents. They rode by on their bikes and would be met with smiles from the family, who spent most of their free time sitting outside.

After a year or two they moved away, and took the banana house with them. When people move away, their trailers usually go with them, removing any evidence they were ever there. All that was left was a cracked concrete driveway. The trailer park was always in flux. Several times a year new dead lots would pop up.

These slabs would always become new hangout spots. Kids would buy supplies and build ramps out of plywood and cinder blocks at either end. They'd scream down the street on their rollerblades and skateboards and bikes, swing into the driveway and hit the ramp, flying into the overgrown grass that now surrounded the driveway. The park manager would have to come through and shew them away like they were raccoons tipping a garbage can. He'd confiscate the ramps and burn them out back by the junk heap.

On the fourth of July people would use the dead lots as a launchpad for fireworks. All of the dads would congregate with their sons, Natty Lights in one hand, M80s in the other. Everyone smelled like cigarettes back then, even if they smoked outside. All the men would walk around shirtless, under the assumption that the smoke from the fireworks would keep the bugs away. They flicked cigarette ashes into a plastic lemon juicer used as a makeshift ashtray. The kids hung around off to the side. The teenagers smoked butts. And the middle schoolers traded cards.

Chris spent that fourth of July with his father. He was standing with a group of kids his age he had never met before. Most of them were kids who lived elsewhere but were getting to spend the holiday with their dads. He stood quietly and listened as they gushed about video games.

Something caught Chris' eye. One of Bill's older brothers was tucked behind the shed next door and he had his hand down a girl's pants. The other boys looked on. They all asked who she was. None of the boys recognized her. Bill's brother must have felt them watching him because he looked right over and locked on Chris. An M80 blast went off and all of the boys ducked. Chris' dad howled and slapped another dad on the shoulder, before he dropped his head back and swallowed another mouthful of beer.

Bill's brother began walking over. "Were you lookin' at me?" He shouted right at Chris. "Huh?"

He walked up to Chris who couldn't make an answer come out of his mouth.

"Wanna smell?" He extended his hand. Chris didn't move. "Go Ahead." He extended his hand until it was almost touching Chris' face.

Chris leans in and reluctantly breathes in. Bill's brother mashed his hand into Chris' face, grabbing his stringy bangs between his fingers. When he pulled his hand away Chris' nose was bloody.

"You mind your own business, you hear me?" He grunted, sounding like his dad.

Chris nodded.

"Good."

A bottle Rocket wizzes into the air.

"Don't tell your dad I gave you that now." He says pointing at his own nose.

Chris wiped a smear of blood across his face, only making it that much more noticeable. Bill's brother walked away and the girl followed after him, avoiding eye contact with the kids. Chris watched as they left. When they were a good distance away the girl went to hold his hand but he ripped it away from her.

Chris' dad whistles. "C'mon now! Get over here."

Chris wiped the rest of the blood off on his shirt and hurried over. "I need you to hold this now alright?" His dad handed him a screamer on a long stick. The stick slumped once it was placed in Chris' hand. "Don't point that at me, alright? Don't point it at anyone." He downs the rest of his beer and tosses the can in a pile. Chris heard a voice say "You listen to your daddy now." But he wasn't sure where it came from.

Chris watched his dad fumble with the lighter. He struck it and nothing lit. "Some bitch." That's what his dad said. "Some bitch" instead of "Son-of-a-bitch". He would also say "Get gone" instead of "Get going". He was the only single dad in the whole park, making him an object of local gossip and pursuit.

One of the other dads leaned in with his cigarette. "Hold'er still." He pressed the cherry to the fuse and it caught. "Alright, hold it straight now. Alright?" Chris' dad crouched down at his side and braced his arm straight up. Chris closed one eye waiting for the screamer to take off.

Nothing happened though. His dad stood back up. "Welp, fuckin dud, I guess. Sorry buddy." Chris shrugged.

"Get gone."

Chris was going to walk back to where all of the other kids had been standing before. None of them were there. He figured maybe they had followed Bill's brother, to get a peak at more action. Or maybe they'd gone to the playground up the street. Chris decided to walk back home.

When he got there a woman was waiting outside their door. She sat on the stoop in a pair of daisy dukes and a tube top.

"Your dad home?"

Chris shook his head no.

She nodded her head knowingly.

"Ah, I knew it... You know how I know?"

Chris listened.

"Cause I'm psychic." She tapped at her temple with a bright pink acrylic nail at the end of her index.

"Really?" Chris asks.

She nods.

"I know all kinds of things. I always know when there's a tv on in the other room. Even when it's on mute.

I can hear it even though other people can't."

Chris didn't know what to say.

She got up from the stoop and walked right up to Chris. "Be better than your dad, alright? Be better than all of 'em." She ran a hand through his hair. This made Chris uncomfortable. He noticed how strong her perfume was, the floral scent dried his mouth out, seeming to replace his spit with flower petals.

ROUGH AIR

Chris would only take one plane flight in his entire life. It happened when he was twenty-five years old. He got the news that his dad had died in a car accident. Drunk driver, not a surprise. Chris and his dad hadn't spoken for a long time and he hadn't cried since receiving the news. But he found himself on a flight back to Florida to bury him and whatever relationship they had.

Chris marveled at all of the gadgets onboard. He played with the air vent overhead, tightening and loosening it to find a comfortable balance. He was excited to browse the movies on the screen in the headrest in front of him, until he realized that there was an extra charge and decided against it. He felt like he was the only one paying attention as the flight attendants were acting out the safety protocol in the aisle. He looked around him at men in cheap button-ups, reading papers or already asleep.

When the plane lifted off, he craned his neck past the sleeping man in the window seat. The ground grew smaller and smaller until it disappeared under cloud cover.

Chris had brought a book to read but found that he couldn't concentrate enough to absorb what he was reading and found himself reading paragraphs two or three times before they registered. He shoved the book back in his carry-on and glanced at the people around him. He wondered about where they were headed and found himself speculating. There was a woman two aisles down who cupped a towel around her face and looked to be breathing deep. He wondered if she was also headed to a funeral. If maybe she was crying under that towel or if it was something else.

He used to make up stories about people when traveling as a kid. When he and his dad still lived alone, together, in that trailer park. His dad would drive him down state to the bigger lakes to go fishing even though he never wanted to. On those long drives Chris would watch the same car drive past them and then fall back for a while before appearing again. He would make up stories about the drivers and passengers. He'd give them whole biographies to keep his mind busy.

About an hour into the flight the plane dropped suddenly, throwing Chris' stomach into his throat. The seatbelt light dinged on and the pilot came over the intercom to let everyone know they'd be hitting more turbulence. "Rough air" is what he called it. This term didn't sit well with Chris. Rough Air. He didn't like the way it sounded and didn't want to feel it come out of his own mouth. Sinus pressure was building behind his right eye, driving him to clench it shut and rub it with his hand. He buried his face in his hoodie as the plane dropped out below him.

Ten minutes later his ears finally popped as they began their descent into Orlando. Chris watched the sprawl of city lights pass by the window.

When the plane landed the tires bounced on the runway before settling. The sound in the cabin peaked as the flaps rose and the plane came to a stop. The entire experience had felt religious to Chris. Some kind of a communal release they'd all experienced. He felt the elation grow inside him. They were all alive and they'd made it together. He let out a laugh of relief as his eyes began to water. He turned to the aisle, hoping to make a connection, to lock eyes with someone else who felt the way that he did. Everyone was checking their phones.

SHARDS

Most of the residents in the trailer park were smokers. They'd sit out on their cinder block stoops and smoke half a pack in the evenings. If the sun was down you could see the cherries glowing red under every carport when you walked by. The butts almost always ended up in a sand-filled coffee tin. They'd crush the butt down in the grains of sand and you'd hear it fizzle out.

Jake and his friends would wait until lights out before making their rounds. They'd pull what was left of the butts from the sand. They'd walk up the street, brushing the remaining sand from the tip of the butts before lighting up and taking the remaining two or three drags. They'd let the cigarettes smolder, hanging from their lips like toothpicks.

Cindy had caught them one night and began

spitefully taking all her butts inside to run them under the faucet before throwing them into her trash can. This earned her a rock through her window.

Jake started stealing beer and smokes from his mom. After she caught him a few times he started buying his own outright from the gas station up the street that never ID'd. If you walked in there with a day's stubble you might as well have been fifty.

One night he broke into the pool house with his friends and smoked weed out of apples. Before they left they smashed all the windows and threw the glass in the pool. There were so many small shards that the property manager had to pay to have the pools drained. He waited for the bottom to dry and a few days later he push-broomed all of the glass into one corner. Little kids hung over the fence asking when the pool would be back open. He'd pause a while before shrugging.

The next day there were stakes hammered into the ground, police tape wrapped around them. The pool was closed for the rest of summer. They wouldn't be filling it back up until the coming spring.

Jake got ambushed and was thrown from the top of the slide. When he hit the ground he landed on his forearm, breaking both bones. After they ran off he laid there, crying awhile. He sat and worried about what to do, putting off his return home because he knew he'd get double beat for either hurting himself or allowing himself to be hurt. He knew his mom would scream in his face. Spit flecks landing here and there, telling him "fight back", because now she'd be working doubles for the next year. He was old enough to know this was all because she was scared. Because she didn't have much in the way of options. Even if he couldn't put it into words.

The hammer never really came down on him so his behavior continued to get worse. The following spring he broke into two trailers. The first one he didn't take anything from. He just lingered in there, knowing they wouldn't be back for a while. He sat in their chair, taking in the different smells. He stared at his curved reflection in the tube tv across from him and tried to imagine himself as someone else. He tried to imagine how these people's lives were different from his own. Unsatisfied, he chose to root around more. He looked through their dressers and tried on their clothes. He ran a toothbrush over his own teeth before returning it to the stand. Before leaving he spun a crock jar full of loose change around, so that the handle was facing away from the room. He'd never get to see the family's reactions but it gave him something to think about. In a week or so they'd notice that something is different and they wouldn't be sure how it got that way and it would have been because of him.

The second house he broke into, he completely decimated. Once he pried the back door open he moved through the trailer like a tornado. He swung open cabinets and drug their contents to the floor. Pushed over the tv and sliced up the furniture. On the way back to his trailer, he pulled feathers from his greasy hair.

His mom was doing dishes on the night he came home covered in blood. She hadn't been able to sleep and had assumed he was asleep in his room. Trying not to make any noise, she rested each dish slowly onto the stack next to her. He came through the door soaked in sweat.

They locked eyes and then she looked down at his cast. The entire thing was covered in dark red gore. Jake crossed his arms and moved to his bedroom. His mom ran after him whispering "What happened?" to herself. He came back in the other direction before she had caught up with him and he shoved her out of his way.

"Where are you going?!" she called after him.

By the time she made it to the front door he was already in the passenger seat of a running car. He slammed the door and she never saw him again.

JUNK HEAP

No one in the trailer park knew how the junk heap had started. Maybe it was there from the beginning, but the turnover in renters was so high that anyone who had witnessed its birth pulled up stakes years prior.

The trash heap sat back at the western corner of the trailer park. The area where only four or five trailers were parked. They sat with great distances between them because there was the space to spare. Not like up front where you could pass a broom between windows. The seclusion of these trailers seemed vast to the park kids. On one hand, privacy seemed like a sign of wealth. The way there are fewer seats, that are larger, in first class on a plane. But on the other hand, kids rarely saw anyone entering and exiting these houses and the longer they hung around that field the more uncomfortable it made them. There was a sinister mystery to those people. It's easy to trust the people up front, no matter how much hell they raised, because they didn't have the room to hide.

Despite the looming fear attached to the area, the kids would inevitably make their way to the heap. Sitting at 30 feet wide and 6 feet tall at its highest point, the heap appeared as a mountain that needed to be conquered. Scattered furniture, outdated appliances, tires & food scraps all made it there. On a rare occasion one of the kids would find a used condom tied off at one end, filled. They'd dare each other to pick it up. Some of them play-acting like they knew what it was. Their voices sounded uncertain, the same way they sounded scared saying the words shit, piss and fuck.

But today wasn't one of those days. Today only one kid hung around the heap. The boy with burs in his hair. He kept to himself and rarely did the other kids seek him out. He walked slowly and methodically along the rusted edges of an old stove. The old appliance quivered under his weight. Letting off a bowing metal sound.

He almost fell when the stray cat burst out from inside the oven. Crouching to hold his balance, he watched as the cat came to a halt and turned to look at him. Half its fur was missing and its left eye was milked over. "Scrawny" he thought, repeating the word in his mind. "Scrawny". At first he was scared but he began feeling bad for the cat. He reached an arm out. Inviting it over. It didn't budge. He slunk down from the stove and began closing the gap. The cat matched his movements, pulling away. Too scared to let him near. He was so locked in on the cat that he didn't even notice his mom pull up in her car. He didn't notice until she cranked down the window and began screaming his name. He looked up. She yelled his name again. Followed by his middle name. Followed by "Don't you touch that cat! I swear to god!" He froze and watched as she got out of the car, leaving the door ajar behind her. She stomped over and grabbed him by the forearm.

"What have I told you about touching those things? Don't you know they might be rabid? Or have fleas?"

"I wasn't going to."

"Don't you lie to me now."

She kept speaking but his eyes drifted from her face and began to follow the cat as it crept toward the open door of the car. Its bones rattled under its skin as it leaned back on its hind legs and hopped inside.

Letting off a high-pitched yelp, she spun one-eighty and made for the car. "Don't you go in there." She said, as if she could still prevent it. The cat stopped, and not thinking, she wrapped her hands around its tail and tried pulling it from the car. The part that stuck with the boy was that much of the cat's hair gave way and ended up in his mother's hands with no resistance. The cat didn't make a sound. It turned to face her. She stared down at all of the calico fur stuck to her palms. She took a step back, afraid to touch it again. Afraid it would crumble in her hands. To her surprise, it hopped out of the car and began to brush her legs. He didn't know what to make of it and neither did his mother. She yelled his name again. Once. And then again followed by his middle name. Followed by "Get in the car now". And like that he was inside the car next to his mother. But something was wrong. She wasn't driving away. She was just sitting there. Her breath was short and rapid. He watched as she lifted her shaking hands up. The fur caked to her hands swayed against her breath. She frantically rolled down her window half-way and scraped her palms against the edge of the window. Her hands were finally clean.

A meow came from outside of her window. She looked out and there was the cat, on its hind legs, at her door, begging to be let in. Begging to be taken home. He couldn't see for sure, but by the way her shoulders were moving he started to think she was crying. He'd never seen his mother cry before. She was always very strong, or more accurately, very angry. But this was different. Something was wrong. And he didn't know what it was. He didn't know what had caused it or how to stop it. It was something more than the cat. Years later he'd always wanted to talk to her about that moment but never knew how to bring it up. And like many things it was left unsaid but not forgotten.

THE UN RAVEL ING

David didn't hang with the boys much. His mom was always a mystery to the other kids. The two of them had moved to the park after her boyfriend, David's dad, ran off on her. She had him young and looked more like an older sister than a mom.

On the rare occasion that the boys went to his trailer, she made them uncomfortable. When they'd come inside, the trailer would always be dark. She'd be balled up in one corner of the couch chain-smoking and crying. The TV always had long movies on, that she would watch all day, back-to-back. *Goodfellas*, *Magnolia*, *The Deer Hunter*. She'd suck back snot and put on a smile for the new guests, waving at the kids, trying not to shake her hand so hard that the ashes would drop from her cigarette. The tears always made her eyes appear exaggerated to them. She would be dressed only in panties and a tank top, nipples visible through the white fabric. When she coughed they would bounce. It was hard for the boys to keep their eyes away. David knew that the other boys looked at her parts. And when they'd get to his room, before any of them could make jokes about it, he'd scold them about how bad it was. How they were being bad friends.

She spent most of her days locked away inside the trailer. Smoking and crying. Polishing off bags of potato chips and sucking the salt from her fingertips. Between movies she would get up and check the dog's bowl to see if she needed to dole out more dry food. The dog was always hiding, but the boys saw evidence of it everywhere. The far corner of the living room was blanketed with newspapers as a makeshift bathroom.

When she left, she'd always dress her version of her best. In one of the sundresses she bought from the KMart. She had one pair of black flats that had seen too many miles. When she wore them she would press bandaids to her achilles to prevent blisters. At the end of the night she would always return home alone.

She would make weekly calls to her mother who spent the time giving her unsolicited advice on how to spend money she knew she'd never have. Her only responses would be "I know mom." or "Thank you, that's very helpful." She'd trained herself to be non-combative to the point of paralysis. That habit probably started around the time that she got pregnant. Her mom spent the majority of those nine months speculating on what-ifs and things she should have done better. After a while she didn't argue. Just nodded.

When David was six he learned how to ride his bike. First with training wheels, but much to her surprise, only one month into having training wheels on his bike he requested she take them off and let him try riding on his own. She did as he requested and as she loosened the bolts she wondered why she was being so cavalier.

She spent that afternoon cheering him on as he rode and fell and eventually found his balance. He rode in circles as she watched him from her stoop clapping her hands. She was happy for the first time in a long time. When she heard it in her own voice it took her aback. She shouted "You're doing so good baby! I'm so proud of you!".

She never made it out of that trailer park. Long after all the boys had grown and left the park she was still there. She went out more often but still came home alone. One night she had too much to drink and drove into the corner of a trailer. The owner came out admonishing her. Shaking a flashlight in her face and demanding she pay for it. Ever conflict averse, she did as he said. Before the police were even called she said it was her fault and began crying on the man's shoulder.

She took up crocheting and got into making large afghans with ornate patterns and she briefly sold them at a church rectory the third weekend of every month, before she grew bored of it and stopped going. She continued to crochet and the afghans piled up in her living room. She didn't mind much. There wasn't much in her trailer at that point and the colors made her feel warm. For brief moments she wasn't plagued by the thought of everything she owned being underwater. That one day half the state would be at the bottom of the Atlantic.

One night, while listening to CNN, she found herself on the floor. It seemed as good a place as any to work on that night's blanket, but the ball of red yarn was out of her reach. She extended her arm and grabbed the loose end between her finger tips and pulled. With each pull the ball unraveled but came no closer. She pulled and pulled, watching the ball grow smaller until there was none left.

SEC URITY SYSTEM

Now that you're older you think a lot about how much time you've wasted. Some of it was out of your control. Some of it was completely your choice. You think about the first ten years of your life. They seem to stretch so long but are filled with so little. That's a third of my life, you think. A third. Ten years is a third of my life. So much of childhood is sitting and observing. You sit and you watch other people live their lives. And then somewhere down the line you begin making your own choices. There's a fear and a guilt attached to those choices. One that never really goes away as you grow.

You forgot about the break-in for a long time. Or you buried it. That feeling of helplessness. Cut off from your parents, asleep in the other room. Strangers inside your house made that 10 foot leap from your bedroom to your mother's an infinite chasm. She never woke during that night and you never slept. Dishes rattling. Plugs yanked from walls. The trailer had thin walls and sound carried into every corner. In the morning she came to realize what happened. When she asks you if you heard anything, you lie. You don't know why. It just escapes your mouth before you can think and now there's no going back. There's no telling her how you hid as still as you could, feeling their eyes on you. Imagining them staring down and seeing through you. Imagining them ripping you up off the bed, knowing you'd be too scared to scream. Not telling her about how helpless you felt.

The following week something comes to your mind. Maybe you were trying to be constructive or maybe you were just scared to be home alone, so soon after being burglarized. Paying for a babysitter wasn't an option. Not on your mother's budget. She would always brag about how mature you were. About how you could handle yourself. You had been cooking all your own meals since you were about 8. And at this point you could cook better than she could. If it didn't come from a box it was either too complicated to make or required too much effort for the sleep schedule she was on.

You pulled out a large bundle of bright red yarn and made for the living room. You're still unsure of where this yarn came from. You'd never known your mother to crochet. With your skinny fingers, you double knot the yarn around the door knob. Triple knot. Then string it across the room, looping it around the leg of an end table. Back across the room to the window lock. Then back around the leg of the couch. On and on. Back and forth until the whole room was strung with bright red lines, zig zagging, keeping you safe. You'd installed a laser security system like you'd seen in so many movies. This would keep you safe. It would keep you both safe.

Years later you can't sleep. You lie in bed and stare up to the popcorned ceiling of your apartment. Your roommates never came home. You assume they're still out or found someone to go home with. The apartment is quiet. Something you're not used to. You sit up and throw on the clothes you wore the previous day. Before you head out you grab that tattered book you've made three attempts to read, giving it another go. The neighborhood is dark and the sidewalk is uneven from the roots growing beneath. But light emanates from just around the corner. The strip of bars you'd spent much of your early twenties in. None of them were particularly nice but the longer you went the more you felt at home. Aspects you'd hated in the beginning now felt familiar.

Attached to one of the bars was a small sandwich shop. Genius idea. Every night, even weekdays, drunks from the surrounding bars would flood in to grab food before stumbling home. It wasn't that late. You could beat the rush and then some. At the counter was a familiar face, a girl who you could swear was making eyes at you whenever you would come in with your girlfriend. You would joke about how dopey she looked and insult her to reassure your girlfriend that you weren't interested. But now that your girlfriend's gone, selfishly, you wish you could get one of those looks again. Just one. You order and wait on your food.

Sitting at the smallest corner table you convince

yourself you'll get that reading done while you wait, but it's karaoke night at the connecting bar and the din is too distracting. It's not strange for you to listen to music while reading but not this loud and not hits from the prior decade. Every song that rises up draws out your memory. You know every lyric even if you can't name the band. You set the book down and give up. A thought crosses your mind. One of relief. You worry what the people around you think. Do you want to be that guy who reads in bars? Who are you? Look at this asshole. Assuming they've all seen you and have formed opinions of you. Fucking asshole.

Your food finally comes and you make a break for home.

When your mom got home, she couldn't understand why you had strung up the house like you did. She opened the door and it snapped back shut. She finally came in the back door. The one they had broken in through, still bent and cracked at the handle. You apologized, thinking it would be obvious to understand your intention. The rest of the day was spent cutting a path through the maze of lanes and untying each knot no matter how tight it had been pulled. You don't recall ever speaking of it again. Even when the next break-in happened months later.

The sight of the knife isn't what threw you off. It was that you couldn't see his mouth moving when he demanded your wallet. "Empty your pockets" he said. "Wow," You thought. "I guess people really say this stuff." And handed everything over including your book and food.

"Where's your phone? Gimme your phone."

"I didn't bring it." Your answer sounded odd. Seeming to give him more information than he needed. Your whole life story in one sentence. He was gone and you weren't sure what to do. You just stood there for a minute. No one else came by. You could hear the pings of the moths bouncing off the humming street lights.

When you got back to the apartment all of the lights were on. Your roommates must have been home. You went around and turned off each one without a second thought. Making your way back down the hall, you stopped. You heard your roommates fucking, quietly, but it was definitely happening. You stopped and thought: "Did I lock the door? This could have been anyone inside my house. House isn't the right word. Home?" Your thoughts trail off as you listen to your roommates fuck. Made comfortable by the familiarity.

B A R
C R A W L

After Bill's first wife left him he bought himself a motorcycle. He had been surprised when they granted his loan, but it was during a recession and they didn't want to turn away paying customers.

He'd ride it to the bar every Friday afternoon to catch up with the friend's who'd stuck around after the divorce. He'd been near sober for the two years he'd been with Megan. She hadn't been much of a drinker so there was rarely alcohol in the house save for holidays and special occasions. But after they'd split he'd found himself bored and lonely. He'd grown accustomed to the constant sound of sharing a space with another person. He began exercising on the dining room floor. Crunches and pushups mostly. He got winded quickly and would lay on his back, flop sweat on his brow. The sound of his breathing would be muffled in his own ears and on occasion he'd feel light-headed.

Bill limited himself to three drinks when he was at the bar. He'd string them out over long hours, ignoring when they became warm from the heat of his hand. Megan was the reason he'd moved to the Midwest. And most of his friends began as her friends. He felt privileged to have them around. He made a conscious effort to remain well-behaved. He didn't want to lose them. In his younger years he had been wild when he drank. His anxiety would flare up and people would find him tossing pressed wood planks onto bonfires. He fell in a fire once and still had the burn scar on his ankle.

He couldn't drink like that anymore. He wasn't sure if it was because of his long spell without it or just getting older. "Maybe both." He'd say to himself, staring down into the pale suds at the bottom of his pint glass. On nights he found himself missing Megan he'd sneak a few extra, telling himself that it was alright. If he was too wobbly to control the bike he'd pull off on a side street that passed by the entrance to the zoo and hang out in the entrance way. Killing the engine and burping up beer foam, cursing himself for not having better control.

The bridge near-by passed over the top of the zoo and people would take walks down the side to stare down at the tigers. They would shout to the animals, trying to get their attention.

One night when Bill was hunkered down in front of the zoo, a couple walked by. Their body language signaled that they were afraid of him. Watching him out to the side of their eyes. Putting their conversation on hold until they passed. As they came up on him, Bill heard the man mutter: "Fuck. You can smell him from here." The girl snickered and added: "Fucking drunky." After they passed the last thing Bill heard was "I bet he's afraid he's going to get pulled over. So he's waiting."

Bill turned the engine over and peeled out. Making sure to maintain eye contact with them the whole time, before he skidded out and ended up with the bike on top of him.

FERAL

Chuck was an oldtimer who lived just inside the entrance to the park. He had a palm tree planted in his front yard that he'd water every evening when the sun had fallen low. It was his ritual. Even when there were water shortages and people were advised to restrict their showers to 5 minutes max. You could find him out there, hose in hand, cigarette between his lips.

His father had been a tough and cruel man. The kind who read a man's calluses when he shook their hands. Never blinking or breaking eye contact. Whenever he hit Chuck he'd always loom over him and declare: "You have to love me. No matter what you're feeling right now. You have to love me. I'm your father."

His mother wasn't much better. Only emboldening her husband's actions with her passiveness. When Chuck would appeal to her to leave his father or express his frustration to her for just standing there and letting it happen, she would usually deflect saying, "You're going to miss me when I'm gone. One day I won't be here anymore and you'll have to think about how poorly you spoke to your mother."

When his father was dying he would sit by his bedside and quietly listen to him speak. His father would try to impart wisdom to him. All of the things he had learned in life. He'd say how getting old was a rich man's thing and that he'd never planned on it. He warned him that some people couldn't be helped, that they were just determined to be the worst kind of person and you couldn't help that. His mind would wander and he would end up making observations that came off more like riddles. One time, staring out the window he croaked: "Staples are packed in boxes, the same as shell casings."

Chuck would be hit with uncanny moments where he'd be looking at how slender his father's wrists had gotten. He would later tell his first wife: "When you spend your whole life being afraid of someone, it's hard to reappraise them as they become weak and die." Something he never told her was that he would find himself fantasizing about smothering his father with a pillow. He wanted this whole process to be done with. He didn't like feeling sympathy for his father. Chuck felt that he hadn't earned it. But he felt too bound to duty and his father passed in his sleep just before Labor Day that year.

Chuck moved down to Florida after that. He got a job halfway to Tampa at a jarring factory. It was good pay but would leave his hand bruised at the end of the week.

The long drive didn't bother him much. He never turned the AC on in his truck, feeling that over time it would save him mounds of money. Mostly he would listen to the wind whip through the window. Whistling and blowing his gray hair in circles.

One morning, before anyone else was on the road, he spotted something on the side of the road as he drove by. Something moving. He pulled over and threw the truck in reverse, riding the shoulder until he came upon what he'd seen. It was a sack with something inside.

When he walked up on the sack he heard a hissing come from inside. The largest cat caught a chunk of his hand as he got the sack open. Blood ran down his thumb as he looked down into the sack of cats. All three of them huddled and hissed at him, hair on end. He reached in slowly to pet them and again. They clawed at him. Not knowing what else to do he tied that sack back up and rested it in the bed of his truck.

He sat for a long minute in the cab of his truck, wiping his hand off with an old tshirt and deciding on what to do with these guys. He felt helpless.

Before lowering the sack into the lake, he apologized to them. He said he was sorry he couldn't do more for them. He said "I'm sorry. You've been made feral from a lack of love. There's nothing I can do. I wish you'd been loved more." Then submerged the sack. Air bubbles rose to the surface and he could feel a thrashing that almost freed the bag. When the fight was over he walked the dripping sack to a dumpster and rested it in gently, closing the lid like a coffin.

AMSCRAY

Kim had the baby. She was living in a small midwest town. Her dad had helped her buy and move into a small fixer-upper, which turned out to be a big fixer-upper. The previous owner hadn't mentioned that the basement flooded every time there was heavy rain. She coated the basement wall's with sealer. When it still leaked she dug out around the entire house and sealed it from the outside as well. Pouring bags and bags of gravel in the gully, convinced it would help with drainage.

The previous owners had two long-haired dogs. She'd spend the next two years pulling tufts of hair from the vents. They'd keep the dogs tied up in the front yard dall day. They never cleaned up after them, and to cover the smell they had planted a huge patch of mint. Its vines snaked through the yard, infectious. It took her two years of mowing over them every weekend to kill them off and allow the grass to fill back in. The vines would get caught around the blades and stall the mower engine out. She'd have to kill the gas, tip the mower over to undo the vines. Every time she did this she pictured the mower coming back to life and taking her hands off.

Kim and her son would sit on the trunk of her car and eat barbecued ribs until they were uncomfortably full. Resting their palms on their stomachs to soothe the food through. Her son would look up at her and match her movements. If she grabbed the collar of her shirt and fluttered it to let the cool air in he'd do the same, but sloppier.

One day he found her digging in the backyard. She sank her shovel into the ground underneath a large oak at the property line. First skimming the layer of grass from the top and setting it aside. Then prying the earth from the hole below. It was the early afternoon and she kept an eye out for neighbors who could see what she was doing. Once the hole reached two feet deep she tossed the shovel aside and strode to the garage. She came back with a paint can that hung low at her side, mostly shielded by her legs. She popped the lid off with the tip of the shovel. There were about two pints of paint left in the bottom of the can. The paint had separated and Kim sloshed it around to recombine it. She poured the paint in the hole and shook the can clean. The garbage company charged extra to dispose of things like old paint and tires. She figured burying it was just as good a solution without the fee. Using her forearm she scooped the dirt back into place, covering the paint. As a finishing touch she sat the grass toupe on top. Squishing it down with her palms. "Good as new" She thought to herself.

When she turned around she saw that her son had been watching her. She didn't know for how long. He was crouched down behind a row of lily plants that had yet to bloom that year.

"How long have you been there?" She called.

He ducked further behind the plant.

"Amscray. Let's make some lunch."

He stood awkwardly, brushing off his knees.

"Amscray!" she said again, with a fake Texas drawl, miming a hand at her side, like she was reaching for a gun in a holster. He giggled and ran for the back door, hands over his head in retreat.

Kim looked back at the tree where she'd buried the paint. When the neighbors noticed the leaves receding from one of the lower limbs they speculated about whether or not the tree was dying. They'd make small talk with her if they were mowing their lawns at the same time. When whole limbs started dying off they'd warn her to not cut under the tree. That they didn't want anything to happen to her. She'd look up at the tree and say: "I guess it's that time. Everything dies off at some point."

Evacuation and *Bruised Palm* previously published in audio form by Hello America Stereo Cassette with backing music by Ted Bizon.

About the Author

Jon Nix is a Filmmaker, Writer and Photographer. He is the director of two feature documentaries. His previous books include *Shy No More* and *The Right Side of Bad*.

He lives in Cleveland, Ohio.

WITH AN

www.ingramcontent.com/pod-product-compliance
Lightning Source LLC
Chambersburg PA
CBHW031542310726
48971CB00008B/2580